"Erin."

His deep voice sent chills along Erin's arms, and brought back a rush of sensation. That hot, pulsing night at the river. Whispered words and shocking pleasure. The devastating sound of goodbye.

His gaze stayed on hers for a moment, then dipped and traveled the length of her. Her pulse tripped, and for a wild second she wished she'd changed into something more appealing. But she'd kept on her faded jeans and sweatshirt to convince herself Wade didn't matter.

His eyes met hers again as the cold wind whipped through the door. He looked tougher than before, stronger. Her gaze lingered on the lean cheeks and hard jaw beneath the stubble, his tanned and sinewed neck.

The lanky, sexy boy she'd loved had become an outrageously appealing man....

Dear Reader,

Well, we're getting into the holiday season full tilt, and what better way to begin the celebrations than with some heartwarming reading? Let's get started with Gina Wilkins's *The Borrowed Ring,* next up in her FAMILY FOUND series. A woman trying to track down her family's most mysterious and intriguing foster son finds him and a whole lot more—such as a job posing as his wife! *A Montana Homecoming,* by popular author Allison Leigh, brings home a woman who's spent her life running from her own secrets. But they're about to be revealed, courtesy of her childhood crush, now the local sheriff.

This month, our class reunion series, MOST LIKELY TO…, brings us Jen Safrey's *Secrets of a Good Girl,* in which we learn that the girl most likely to…*do everything* disappeared right after college. Perhaps her secret crush, a former professor, can have some luck tracking her down overseas? We're delighted to have bestselling Blaze author Kristin Hardy visit Special Edition in the first of her HOLIDAY HEARTS books. *Where There's Smoke* introduces us to the first of the devastating Trask brothers. The featured brother this month is a handsome firefighter in Boston. And speaking of delighted—we are absolutely thrilled to welcome RITA® Award nominee and Red Dress Ink and Intimate Moments star Karen Templeton to Special Edition. Although this is her first Special Edition contribution, it feels as if she's coming home. Especially with *Marriage, Interrupted,* in which a pregnant widow meets up once again with the man who got away—her first husband—at her second husband's funeral. We know you're going to enjoy this amazing story as much as we did. And we are so happy to welcome brand-new Golden Heart winner Gail Barrett to Special Edition. *Where He Belongs,* the story of the bad boy who's come back to town to the girl he's never been able to forget, is Gail's first published book.

So enjoy—and remember, next month we continue our celebration….

Gail Chasan
Senior Editor

Please address questions and book requests to:
Silhouette Reader Service
U.S.: 3010 Walden Ave., P.O. Box 1325, Buffalo, NY 14269
Canadian: P.O. Box 609, Fort Erie, Ont. L2A 5X3

WHERE HE BELONGS

GAIL BARRETT

SPECIAL EDITION

Published by Silhouette Books

America's Publisher of Contemporary Romance

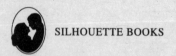 SILHOUETTE BOOKS

ISBN 0-373-24722-2

WHERE HE BELONGS

Copyright © 2005 by Gail Ellen Barrett

Books by Gail Barrett

Silhouette Special Edition

Where He Belongs #1722

GAIL BARRETT

always dreamed of becoming a writer. After living everywhere from Spain to the Bahamas, raising two children and teaching high school Spanish for years, she finally fulfilled that lifelong goal. Her writing has won numerous awards, including Romance Writers of America's prestigious Golden Heart. Gail currently lives in western Maryland with her two sons, a quirky Chinook dog and her own Montana rancher turned retired Coast Guard officer hero. Write to her at P.O. Box 65, Funkstown, Maryland 21734-0065, or visit her Web site, www.gailbarrett.com.

Dear Reader,

What a pleasure this is to introduce you to my debut
novel, *Where He Belongs,* and especially to its hero,
Wade Winslow. From the moment I began writing
this book, Wade intrigued me, not only because of his
smoke-jumping career and daring lifestyle, but because
he's a real hero—a man who can't help but do the right
thing, even at his own expense.

Like Wade, I grew up in a small town. And also like
Wade, I spent years traveling and living in different
places. But I've learned that while moving can be
exciting, it also has a cost, the loss of roots and a
sense of belonging.

Now Wade has his own lessons to learn. He must return
to his hometown, confront his painful past and listen to
his heart—because only love can show him where he
belongs. I hope you enjoy his journey.

Gail Barrett

Chapter One

Wade Winslow wanted only one thing as he cranked the throttle on his Harley V-Rod and rumbled down the main street of Millstown, Maryland—to get the hell back out. Millstown. His home sweet hometown, where he was White Trash Winslow, no matter how many years had passed. Where bad reputations lingered longer than the antebellum town houses lording over the narrow street. Where even the ancient oak trees sneered down at him, their twisted branches reaching out like fingers of condemnation, trapping him in the past.

Battling the urge to kick up a gear and blast himself back into sanity, he tightened his grip on the throttle. Norm. He had to reach Norm. That goal had driven him for the past two days, straight from Miami, ever since he'd gotten the message that the cancer had spread and the man who'd taken him in as a kid lay dying. *Dying.* Hell. Didn't anyone he loved survive?

With dread settling deep in his gut, he downshifted at the Stone Mill Café, edged into the narrow alley beside the abandoned theater, and turned the wrong way onto the one-way street that served as a shortcut through town. Then he twisted back on the throttle and rocketed to the end of the lane, the roar of the engine matching his mounting frustration.

Norm had lived out of town back then, on a few rocky acres tucked against South Mountain on the fringes of Appalachia. A lousy farm, but the perfect place to teach a rebellious kid to survive. But Norm had sold the farm and moved into town when Rose died and Wade had left, and the smoking finally caught up to him.

At the end of the road, Wade dropped a gear and pulled into the driveway beside the duplex Norm called home. He parked the Harley beside a row of cars in the driveway, hooked his helmet over the backrest and straightened his aching body. Then he raked back his hair and tucked in the T-shirt he wore under his leather jacket. Sick or not, Norm didn't tolerate disrespect. And he was the one man Wade owed too much to ever defy.

And now he was going to lose him.

His nerves tight, he strode to the door and entered a small, coffee-scented kitchen packed with neighbors: Jack Fleagle, who'd run the theater before it closed; Mrs. Cline, retired from the post office last year. And Battle-Ax Bester, a linebacker of a woman with a rigid, beehive hairdo. Good God. As if he didn't have enough to contend with.

Her crayoned lips curled down. "You have some nerve showing up."

Hell. A dozen years after high school and she still acted as if he'd kill a man and end up in prison like his father. No wonder he hated this town.

"Wade, you made it." Norm's younger brother, Max, in his fifties himself now, stepped around Mrs. Bester and reached out his hand.

Wade shook it and caught the tension in his eyes. His stomach dipped. "He hasn't—"

"No." Max clapped his shoulder. "Go on back. The nurse is there, but he's been asking to see you."

With foreboding weighting his steps, Wade threaded his way through the crowd and headed down the hall to Norm's bedroom. He tapped on the door and pushed it open. "Norm?"

A woman he didn't know turned toward him. "Excuse me, but Mr. Decker needs to—"

"Wade," Norm wheezed. "You came…"

Wade's heart stalled as the nurse moved away from the bed, and he forced himself to breathe. Good God. Was that Norm? Glazed eyes stared out from his bloodless face. Wrinkled skin sagged from his bones, as withered as the dry leaves clinging to the oak trees outside.

Sick dread speared his gut. What happened? Norm had looked fine last spring when he'd stopped on his way to Montana.

"You can only stay a minute," the nurse warned. "He just took his medicine. If you need anything, I'll be in the kitchen."

"So what's with the Mr. Decker bit?" Struggling to

mask his shock, Wade pulled a straight-backed chair close to the bed and eased himself down. "You putting on airs now that you live in town? Hell, if I'd known you were getting formal, I'd have worn a suit."

"Heard the bike. Knew you'd come…"

Damn right he'd come, instantly, stopping only for a few hours to sleep at the North Carolina border.

"Where…?"

"Florida. Found a great beach. You wouldn't believe the babes down there."

"Not…California?"

Still reeling, he fought to keep his tone light. "Nah. I went to San Diego as soon as the fire season ended, but the traffic got to me. It's one big freeway from L.A. to the border now. So I headed to Florida instead. Thought maybe I'd fly to the Bahamas and hide out for a while." And let his wrecked knee heal so he wouldn't lose his smokejumping job. He stretched out his throbbing leg.

"Hurt?"

He grimaced. Cancer had ravaged Norm's body, but not his mind. "Jolted my knee. Hit some down air on my last jump and landed hard. Nothing serious. I had to hike over the mountain after we got the fire out, though, so it could use a rest."

Norm closed his eyes. "Good place, Millstown. Stay…" He winced, then wheezed.

Wade's heart lunged. "What's wrong? Should I call the nurse?"

"No." He opened his glassy eyes. "Damn morphine…"

Wade glanced at the morphine pump hanging from the IV bag. The oxygen tank beside the bed. The wheelchair in the corner. Props to ease the descent into death. He tried to speak but failed. He swallowed hard.

Norm's mouth moved and he leaned closer to catch the words. "Stay…"

"I'd planned on it."

"Promise. Need you to…"

Norm wasn't asking him to live in Millstown. He always knew Wade couldn't stay. He just wanted him here when he died. *Died.* Oh, God.

"You need me to what? Cook you Thanksgiving dinner? Hell, Norm. Next thing I know you'll be wanting me to polish the silver." Like when Rose was alive. Panic surged, then buzzed in his head.

"Not here. Promise me, Wade…"

He was going to lose Norm. Oh God, no. Not Norm, too.

"Wade…"

Sweat formed on his brow. He couldn't take this. Norm dying. Staying in Millstown. But he couldn't leave. He couldn't let down Norm. "I'll be here." For as long as he needed him.

"Not here," Norm repeated.

"What's not here?"

"Rent…room…"

Rent a room? He frowned. What was he saying? "I'm not leaving you, Norm." His heart jerked at the thought. "I'll crash on the couch, same as I always do."

"No." Norm's voice was suddenly sharp. "Nurse is here. Max. Need you to stay…Mills Ferry…"

Mills Ferry? The old mansion on the outskirts of town? Why would he stay there? And why would Norm want him to? Unless….

His shoulders stiffened. "What am I, company now? Is that it? I'm not wel—"

"No, Wade." Norm's hand snaked from beneath the sheet and grabbed his wrist. The slight weight trembled cold on his skin. "Son. Always my son… Need help. Please…" His voice faded.

Dread knifed through Wade's gut. "But—"

"Promise me. Promise…" Norm's hand slid from his wrist.

His lungs squeezed shut. He'd do anything for this man, no matter how odd the request. "Fine, I'll stay there."

"Good." Norm slumped back and closed his eyes.

"Norm? Norm?"

"Sir?" The nurse spoke from behind him. "Mr. Decker needs to rest now."

He sucked in a shallow breath. Norm hadn't died. He was just sleeping, thank God.

But for how much longer?

His legs unsteady, he stood. Norm had always seemed invincible to Wade, a big, burly man with thick arms and calloused hands. A quiet man who taught him to track and shoot deer. How to rebuild the truck he rolled when he took that curve too fast, and what to do when the girls started calling.

A calm, patient man who'd lost his temper only once in all those years, when Wade had smarted off to Rose. Wade had never done it again.

And now that strong man lay dying.

"Sir?"

A deep ache gutting his chest, he moved to the foot of the bed. His eyes burned as the nurse slipped the oxygen mask over Norm's face and adjusted the pillows.

And suddenly he couldn't take it anymore. He needed space. Air. He strode from the room and straight through the crowded kitchen.

"Wade. Hey, Wade!"

He shoved open the door and stalked outside. Damned cancer! He jerked his helmet off his bike and dragged it over his head. How could it spread that fast? And why hadn't Max called him sooner? He yanked on his leather gloves.

"Wade, wait up."

He straddled the Harley, then scowled at Max, who'd followed him outside. "Why didn't you tell me he'd had a relapse?" he demanded. "I've got money, for God's sake. I could have taken him to Baltimore to a specialist instead of using that quack out here."

"He's been seeing a specialist. At Johns Hopkins. He's been going there for over a year."

His stomach plunged. "And you didn't tell me?"

"I wanted to. We all did, but Norm convinced us to wait."

"I see." And suddenly he did. Clearly. The whole town had known Norm was dying and no one had bothered to tell him.

"We thought, well, with everything else you've been through…" Max spread his hands. "We didn't want you to worry."

"Right." He snapped down the visor on his helmet, cranked the key in the Harley's ignition and revved the engine. Like hell they didn't want him to worry. They didn't tell him because he wasn't family. Because he didn't belong here. Never had, never would.

Because in Millstown, nothing changed. He rammed the bike into gear and shot off.

The cold wind gusted across the Potomac River, thrashing the woods at Mills Ferry and rattling the stone mansion's windows. Erin McCuen leaned against the bubbled glass and shivered. She couldn't put it off any longer. She had to turn up the heat before her grandmother got sick.

Desperation surged but she ruthlessly quelled it. She couldn't panic, no matter how deep in debt she was sinking. Somehow she'd pay those bills.

"Did you go to the bank?" her grandmother asked from the chair beside her.

"Yes, Grandma." She sighed. "Everything's fine."

"…stealing my money. They think I don't know."

"Don't worry. The bank account's just how you left it." Empty, and likely to stay that way. She glanced at the red bird perched on the feeder outside the window. "Look, a cardinal. I think those sunflower seeds did the trick."

She helped her grandmother hold the binoculars in her trembling hands so she could get a closer look. Thank goodness cardinals didn't migrate. Her grandmother had lost so much in the car wreck—some speech and motor skills, short-term memory, the ability to make her beloved quilts. Watching birds from her sunroom was the only pleasure she had left.

And Erin was going to make sure her grandmother could watch those birds from the security of her home until she died—no matter how dire their finances.

Pushing back the familiar swell of anxiety, she set the binoculars aside. Then she picked up the faded quilt from a nearby chair and wrapped it around Grandma's shoulders. Ever since that accident, the bills had mounted. Medicare covered the bulk, thank goodness, but without a supplement, she had to pay the rest. And while she struggled through the insurance nightmare, submitting claims and juggling payments, her historic home rotted away. She couldn't begin to fund the repairs that money pit demanded.

So she'd started tutoring after teaching high school all day. She'd slashed expenses, sold furniture and even mortgaged Mills Ferry, the family's estate for ten generations. In desperation, she'd borrowed money from their neighbor, Norm Decker. Still, the bills piled up.

Her stomach roiled. She was frugal by nature and any debt made her nervous. Hovering on the edge of bankruptcy like this drove her wild. But what could she do? Even small changes confused her grandmother and agitated her for days. Losing her home would destroy her.

So she struggled to hold on to the house. But unless a miracle happened soon…

She heard the front door close and she patted her grandmother's shoulder. "Lottie's here, Grandma. You keep watching the cardinal. I'll be back as soon as I set out dinner."

She crossed the front parlor they used as their family room and entered the spacious foyer. She'd closed off most of the house after the accident to cut utility bills—the attic and cellar, every spare bedroom, the dining room and entire third floor. She'd moved her grandmother into the first floor library for easier access, and herself into the smallest bedroom upstairs.

She'd also tried to rent out the master bedroom. Unfortunately, Millstown didn't attract tourists and no one had answered her ad.

"It's getting cold out there." Lottie removed her long, woolen coat and looped it over the coat tree in the entry. "If this keeps up, we'll get snow for Thanksgiving."

"I sure hope not." With their ongoing drought, they needed the moisture, but snow meant higher heating bills, which she couldn't afford.

Lottie removed her beret and fluffed out her short, gray curls. "I put your mail on the hutch."

"Thanks, Lottie. I appreciate it." She glanced at the basket heaped with bills and rubbed the insistent throb in her forehead.

"Another headache?"

"I'm fine." She forced a smile. A retired nurse, Lottie had moved into their renovated spring house when her husband died. In exchange for room and board, she cared for Grandma while Erin worked. And she was a godsend. Erin couldn't have managed without her.

She headed into the kitchen. "The casserole's ready. I hope you don't mind tuna again."

"Tuna's fine, but I thought you were going out with Mike tonight."

"No time. I've got essays to correct."

"You keep turning that man down and he's going to lose interest," Lottie scolded from behind her. "He's a good man, too, something you can't take for granted these days."

Erin grabbed the hot pads from the counter and opened the oven door. Lottie was right. Mike was a good man, the type who'd cheerfully settle down and support a family. And she enjoyed talking to him at work. A lot. But she didn't have time to date these days. "He's got his own grades to do. He understands."

"Maybe, but you still need to relax. You're always working and volunteering."

"Being busy isn't a crime."

"No, but people take advantage of you, hon. The town won't fall apart if you say no for once."

She removed the casserole from the oven, set it on the counter and took out the side dish of beans. So she did more than her share. She didn't mind. She loved helping her community.

Lottie sighed and opened the silverware drawer. "Well, don't blame me when you drop from exhaustion. By the way, I stopped at Norm's on the way home."

"How is he?"

"Not good."

A heavy feeling weighted her heart. Norm was her grandmother's closest friend and the most generous person she knew. She couldn't bear to think of him dying.

"At least Wade made it here in time," Lottie said.

Wade. Erin froze and for long seconds struggled to breathe. Lottie couldn't know, she told herself desperately. No one knew, aside from herself and Wade. Lottie was just making conversation.

"That's good." She carefully hung the hot pads on the hook beside the stove and prayed that her voice sounded normal.

"And Norm said he's staying with us."

"What?" Erin's mind blanked. "Who's staying with us? Norm?"

"No, of course not. Wade is." Lottie pulled out the silverware and closed the drawer. "Norm asked about the room the other day, but I forgot to tell you. I assumed it was fine since you keep running that ad."

Erin's heart tripped, then careened through her chest. Wade would be in her house? Renting her room? *Wade?*

"In fact, he'll probably be here soon," Lottie added. "I'll set an extra place in case he's hungry."

Erin gaped at Lottie. Wade was on his way here?

Lottie cocked her head to the side. "Are you okay, hon?"

She blinked. "I'm fine. I just…I mean, I'd better check the room. Make sure the vent's open so he'll get heat. Do you mind helping Grandma?"

Lottie waved her off. "Go on. I'll get Mae."

Erin whirled from the kitchen. She took the stairs two at a time, rushed into the master bedroom and slammed the door. Then she leaned against the wall and gasped for breath.

Wade Winslow. Here. In her house.

Oh, Lord.

She placed her palm over her heart and dragged in a steadying breath. She had to get a grip. Wade had happened years ago. Twelve long years ago. One incredible, passionate night that had meant the world to her and nothing to him.

Not that she'd blamed him. She'd always known he wouldn't stay. Even though she had hoped….

But she wasn't the type to delude herself. Not then, and certainly not now. Especially when it came to Wade Winslow.

She straightened and crossed to the bed. Reaching up, she removed a picture frame from the wall. Then, for an endless moment, she gazed at the wrinkled paper inside and let herself drift to the past. Wade's poem. That night. The sound of him driving away.

A huge ache lodged in her chest, that painful mix of longing and passion, sympathy and desolation that comprised her feelings for Wade.

Then she sighed. More than a decade had passed since then, and Wade was just an old friend now, a former high school classmate. A houseguest, whose rent would help pay her bills.

And she could handle him. She could. She marched to the dresser and stuck the frame beneath the quilt in the bottom drawer. She opened the heating vent, straightened the bedspread, and hung clean towels in the bathroom. Satisfied, she walked to the bedroom door.

And stopped. Handle him? Wade Winslow? Who was she fooling?

Oh, Lord. She'd better hold tight to her heart.

Chapter Two

Wade raced along the road that fronted the Potomac River, banking hard into the corners and venting the anger that simmered in his gut. By the time he slowed to cross the one-lane bridge at Mills Ferry, his temper had subsided into frustration.

Why had Norm hidden the truth from him? Why hadn't Max told him how sick Norm was? And how in the hell could he fix it now?

His stomach knotted, he pulled into the turnout in the woods below Mills Ferry and cut the engine. Then he tugged off his helmet and scowled out at the leaden river. A ribbon of sparrows dipped over the water, twisting, contracting, and finally swooping away until the black specks merged with the tombstone-gray sky—the same damn color as the rocks, river and everything else in this blasted town.

A fierce ache cramped his throat and he tipped back his head and shut his eyes. Hell. The place even smelled like death-parched earth and rotting leaves. The same stench as when his mother died, and later Rose.

Fighting back the painful lump in his throat, he forced his mind to the bare branches creaking against the moan of wind in the pines, the weariness seeping through his body. When the cramp in his chest eased slightly, he again opened his eyes.

He needed to sleep. That was his problem. He was just too drained to think straight anymore. In the morning, when his head was clear, he could find a way to help Norm.

He cranked the key in the Harley's ignition and felt it rumble to life. Not bothering to put on his helmet, he pulled back onto the road and drove the quarter mile to the ridge. He still couldn't believe Norm wanted him to stay at Mills Ferry. Since when did Mrs. McCuen rent rooms? And what if he ran into Erin?

His gut clenched at that possibility, but he pushed aside the thought. No way was he dwelling on Erin. He had enough on his mind without going down that road tonight.

He stopped at the mansion's iron gates and idled the engine, then scanned the small, hand-lettered sign advertising a room. So Norm was right. But why was Mrs. McCuen taking in renters? He never thought she'd need the money.

Still mulling that over, he turned onto the long gravel drive lined with oak trees and threaded his way toward the house. Potholes and dangling branches threatened to knock him off his bike, and he felt more off kilter.

Growing up, Mills Ferry had represented everything he didn't have: history, tradition, old-world society and wealth. And it was a showcase. The trim was kept freshly painted and flowers bloomed everywhere. But dried leaves blew across the rutted driveway and heaped against the stone fences now.

He parked his Harley at the end of the driveway beside a faded blue Honda Civic. With a groan, he rolled his shoulders and stretched, then climbed off the bike and hefted the saddlebag over his shoulder.

God, he was tired. And his knee had stiffened up again. He limped slowly around the giant azalea bushes spilling over the gravel and climbed the front porch steps. The warped boards bent and creaked beneath his feet.

Shaking his head, he crossed to the massive front door and pushed the bell. When it didn't ring, he braced his hands on his hips. What was with this place? He couldn't imagine Mrs. McCuen letting it go like this. Unless she'd sold it? But that was even less likely.

Frowning, he looked across the sagging porch to a broken tree limb in the yard and a sick feeling rose in his gut. All these years he'd kept a picture in his mind of Erin standing here on the porch—beautiful, secure in her elegant mansion, untouched, except for that night at the river. But what if she wasn't so safe? What if he had been wrong?

Guilt surged, but he shoved it aside. He was definitely not going down that track, he reminded himself. Erin and Mills Ferry were none of his business. The only thing he needed to worry about tonight was sleep.

He turned back to the door, lifted the clawed knocker

and slammed it down. Then he leaned his forearm against the doorjamb to wait.

The sharp rap on the door jerked Erin's heart to a halt. For several long seconds she clutched her napkin, unable to move, unable to think.

"That must be Wade," Lottie said cheerfully. "I'll get it."

"Oh, no, that's okay." Her heart suddenly hammering, she scraped back her chair and rose from the kitchen table. "I'll let him in. I'll need to show him the room, make sure he knows where the towels are, explain the meals…"

She was rambling. Avoiding Lottie's perceptive gaze, she set her napkin beside her plate and squeezed her grandmother's hand. "I'll be right back, Grandma."

She exited the kitchen and walked quickly down the hall to the foyer, her heart drumming louder than her footsteps on the wood floor. This was silly, she told herself firmly. She could act normal for the short time he was here. After all, he had nothing to do with her life anymore.

Summoning an image of herself as calm, friendly neighbor, she took a deep breath and opened the door. Her breath jammed in her throat.

Wade dominated the doorway, one leather-clad forearm braced on the frame, the other hand propped on his hip. He was taller than she remembered, broader through the shoulders and chest, and far more muscular than he'd been as a teen. But his short, shaggy hair was the same chestnut-brown, along with the stubble that lined his hard jaw.

Her gaze collided with those familiar, whiskey-colored eyes and her pulse fluttered madly. They were the eyes of a man who'd expected nothing from the world and gotten less. Bleak, cynical eyes set in a face etched with pain and exhaustion.

She swallowed hard. "Wade."

"Erin." His deep voice raised chills along her arms and brought back a rush of sensation. That hot, pulsing night at the river. Whispered words and shocking pleasure. The devastating sound of goodbye.

His gaze stayed on hers for a moment, then dipped and traveled the length of her. Her pulse tripped and for a wild second she wished she'd changed into something more appealing. But she'd kept on her faded jeans and sweatshirt to convince herself Wade didn't matter.

His eyes met hers again as the cold wind whipped through the door. He looked tougher than before, stronger. Her gaze lingered on the lean cheeks and hard jaw beneath the stubble, his tanned and sinewed neck. The lanky, sexy boy she'd loved had become an outrageously appealing man.

He tilted his head. "Norm said something about a room?"

"Oh, of course." Her face warmed. "I'm sorry. It's just such a surprise to see you that I… Come in." Silently berating herself for gawking like the lovestruck girl she'd once been, she moved back to let him pass.

He straightened and stepped through the door and she pushed it shut behind him. While his gaze swept the foyer, she rushed to fill the silence. "You're my first guest, so you'll have to excuse me if I seem a bit flustered."

His gaze narrowed on hers. "You still live here?"

"Of course. I always intended to stay." Did that sound too accusing? Her face warmed even more. "Besides, after I started teaching, there wasn't any point in moving. I mean, where else would I live in Millstown? And then after the accident…"

Noting the weary set to his shoulders, she stopped. A surge of remorse flooded through her. Here she was rambling on about herself when he was clearly exhausted.

And suffering. Norm meant everything to Wade. He'd endured a childhood filled with death and rejection, especially when his father went to prison. Norm was one of the few who'd cared about the abandoned boy. She had been another.

"Listen, Wade. I'm really sorry about Norm." She reached out to touch his arm but the hard set of his jaw warned her off. She dropped her hand to her side.

Wade had never wanted her sympathy, never even allowed her close—except for that night at the river. But if the boy had been adept at hiding emotions, this man had become an expert.

"I'll need you to sign the register," she said, taking refuge in a safer topic. She crossed the foyer to the hutch, opened a drawer and pulled out a clipboard and pen. "You can pay by the night or the week, which is a little cheaper. Breakfast is included with the room, but you can have full board if you want, although truthfully, lunch is just leftovers or sandwiches since I'm gone during the day."

When he strode toward her, she noticed his limp. No surprise there. Anyone who made a living jumping out of airplanes was bound to get injured. And Wade always had taken more risks than most.

He reached for the clipboard and she saw scars on his hands. "The rates are at the bottom," she said as he scanned it. "But you get a ten percent discount since you're a friend."

"I don't care about the cost." He scribbled his name on the paper and handed it back.

"Fine." She set the clipboard back in the drawer. "The kitchen is just down the hall." Of course, he would remember that. "We're eating now. If you're hungry, you're welcome to join us."

"No, thanks. I'd rather sleep."

She nodded and started up the curving staircase. "Well, if you get hungry later, help yourself to any leftovers you find in the fridge. You can heat them up in the microwave. My grandmother sleeps in the room off the kitchen, but she doesn't hear well anymore, so don't worry about bothering her. I'm up here, just down the hall from you."

She glanced back to make sure he was following. Despite the limp, he climbed the stairs quickly and she was struck again by his strength. She'd never quite believed Norm's renditions of Wade's smokejumping escapades—lugging a hundred-pound pack over steep mountains, carrying an injured buddy to safety. But judging by the width of those shoulders, she fully believed Norm now.

At the landing she crossed to the master bedroom, then waited inside for him to catch up. She'd always loved this room with its original, random-width flooring, the gorgeous fireplace mantel and bay windows overlooking the river.

But Wade wasn't here to admire the scenery.

He dropped his bag on the braided rug, pulled off his leather jacket and tossed it on the bed. Her gaze traveled from his heavily corded arms to his flat stomach, up his wide, muscled chest to his face. When he pinched the space between his eyebrows, her heart rolled. The man was clearly exhausted.

"The bathroom's straight through there." She pointed past the armoire. "If you need anything, just let me know."

When he didn't answer, she turned to leave. She grabbed the door to close it behind her, hesitated and glanced back. "I might not be here when you get up in the morning, so help yourself to anything you want in the kitchen. The coffee should be on. I usually leave the front door unlocked since Lottie's here with Grandma, but I'll set an extra key for you on the hutch."

She shut the door behind her and walked to the stairs, then stopped and clutched the railing. Her pulse heaved in her ears. Her knees trembled and threatened to buckle. *Oh, Lord.* As a teen, she'd adored Wade Winslow—his wild and reckless ways, his raw masculinity, the tough attitude that hid his soft heart. But this man…

She sucked in a reedy breath. The adult Wade Winslow rattled her completely.

And she had to be brutally honest. No matter how many years had passed, he still affected her. Always had and probably always would. But the grown man didn't want her sympathy or love any more than the boy had. Maybe less.

Sighing deeply, she headed down the stairs. Wade

had built barriers around his heart, all right, formidable ones that she'd never breach. Not that it mattered. Once Norm died, he'd leave, the same as he did before. Only this time, he'd never return.

Wade braced his hands on the shower wall and angled his head so the hot water pummeled his shoulders. He groaned as the heat seeped into his muscles and eased the stiffness and pain. After twelve hours of sleep and a shower, he felt almost human.

Not that feeling tired was new. Despite napping every chance he got—on the jump plane en route to a fire, on a folding chair in the ready-room, or even in a patch of shade on the tarmac—he lived with chronic exhaustion. And filth. Fighting wildfires was dirty work. He routinely spent days digging fire lines, falling snags with his chain saw and sifting through ashes for hot spots, all in the same, sweat-drenched clothes.

But as good as this shower felt, he didn't have time to linger. Snapping off the water, he toweled off and pulled on a T-shirt and jeans. Then he tossed the quilt over the rumpled sheets on the bed and quickly jerked on his jacket. Max would have called if anything had happened to Norm, but he couldn't afford to waste time.

The hot water had worked the stiffness from his knee, so he tramped easily down the wide, winding staircase and through the back hall to the kitchen. He wondered if Erin was still around. That had been a shock last night, finding her in the doorway.

She'd looked more fragile than he remembered, thinner, but still beautiful with that thick, auburn hair piled carelessly on her head. He'd seen that same, deep red in crown fires over the years. The color never failed to mesmerize him, reminding him of Erin's long, gleaming hair streaming over her naked breasts in the moonlight.

He never understood why she'd come to him that night. It still seemed like his wildest dream. She hadn't hung out with that crowd, shouldn't even have been at that party. And when she'd kissed him, touched him, begging him to make love to her, she'd shocked him out of his mind.

He should have walked away. A decent man would have done that. But he'd ached for her, hungered for her for so damn long that he couldn't deny himself—or her, when she'd whispered his name. He'd never had the heart to turn down Erin.

But no matter how incredible that night had been, Erin wasn't his business now. He'd only come back to help Norm—which he intended to do as soon as he grabbed some coffee.

He entered the large, farm-style kitchen. Long counters flanked a deep sink topped with tall windows. Mrs. McCuen and another woman he vaguely recognized sat at a table drinking coffee. When he didn't see Erin, he hitched out his breath.

"Hello, Wade." The woman with the wispy gray hair smiled. "I'm not sure if you remember me. I'm Lottie Brashears. I was the school nurse for a while."

"Sure, I remember." He nodded to Erin's grand-mother, a tiny woman with white hair piled on her head. "Mrs. McCuen."

Mrs. McCuen frowned. "Are you from the bank?"

"The bank? No."

"You remember Wade, don't you?" Lottie asked her. "Norm Decker's boy. He went to school with Erin."

Mrs. McCuen's expression eased. "Oh, yes, Erin's friend."

Friend. Right. The friend who took her virginity and then fled town. But he'd been right to leave. Erin deserved someone better than him. Someone respectable, stable, who'd keep her happy and safe.

He shifted his gaze to the counter. "Mind if I have some coffee?"

"Go right ahead," Lottie said. "The cups are above the machine. Help yourself to the doughnuts, too. Or there's cereal, if you'd rather have that."

"This is great, thanks." He filled a mug with black coffee, stacked three glazed doughnuts on a napkin, and headed to the table. He hooked a chair with his foot, pulled it out and sat.

"I'll bet Norm's glad you're back," Lottie said. "He always hoped you'd settle down here."

A bite of doughnut stuck in Wade's throat and he washed it down with coffee. "I'm not staying long," he said when he'd swallowed. "I'm just here to see Norm."

"Oh, I see," Lottie said as if she really didn't. He frowned. He didn't owe anyone in this town explanations. Besides, he had a great life out west, making good money at a job he loved.

"Well, anyway, it's nice of you to visit," she said. "Norm's a good friend. He really helped Mae after the accident."

Wade glanced at Mrs. McCuen. Her hand trembled, slopping coffee over the cup. "Erin mentioned an accident last night."

Lottie settled Mae's cup on the saucer and blotted the spill with a napkin. "Mae hit a patch of ice last winter at the intersection with the highway and broadsided a truck. It was touch and go for a while, but she's come through all right." She smiled and patted Mae's hand.

"A nuisance," Mrs. McCuen said.

"You're no such thing," Lottie countered. She looked at Wade to explain. "I keep Mae company while Erin works. She needs a little help getting around."

Wade's gaze settled on Erin's grandmother. A little help? The woman could barely drink her coffee unassisted.

He drained his own cup and rose for a refill. "So Erin teaches now?"

"History at St. Michaels Academy."

That fit. He could see her in front of a classroom exalting the virtues of historic Millstown, though not in a private school. She'd never been a snob, despite her family's background. Hell, she'd even been nice to him.

He snagged another doughnut and gazed out the window over the sink. Downed tree limbs poked through the ragged lawn. He thought of the sagging front porch and unease built in his gut.

"Erin's a good teacher," Mrs. McCuen said carefully.

"You bet she is," Lottie agreed. "They're darned lucky to have her. I've never seen anyone work so hard."

An image of Erin rose in Wade's mind, her green

eyes lined with shadows. He slugged back his coffee and frowned. He didn't want to think of Erin suffering. He wanted her insulated from the rough side of life— just the way he'd left her.

"My fault," Mrs. McCuen whispered.

"It's not your fault," Lottie scolded. "Accidents happen. Don't even think of blaming yourself. Besides, Wade's here to help us now."

"What?" He turned.

"Oh, I didn't mean you had to do anything. Erin would never want that. But now that you're renting that room, she can hire out some of those chores."

Erin needed money to fix the house? Is that why Norm sent him here? Oh, hell. "I'm not staying long. A week, maybe two. It all depends on Norm."

"Oh, I'm sure Erin realizes that."

"I work in Montana now."

"Yes, Norm told us about your adventures. You're quite the hero around here." Lottie rose to clear the table.

Hero? He mentally scoffed. He did his job like any smokejumper. And that's exactly what he was, a smokejumper. They couldn't seriously expect him to stay

Not even to help Erin? The churning in his stomach grew.

He put his cup in the sink. "Look, let's get this straight. I don't know what Norm told you, but I'm not moving back to Millstown. I'm not even staying here long. Now, thanks for the coffee, but I've got to go."

"Say hi to Norm for us," Lottie called as he left the kitchen.

His agitation mounting, he strode to the front of the house. Once outside, he paused on the porch to zip his jacket. Bushes sprawled over the railing. Peeling paint glistened in the frosty air. He looked at the rutted driveway and the sick feeling blew into panic.

He wasn't staying in Millstown. He couldn't! Damn Norm anyway. Exactly what was he trying to do?

He stomped down the steps, determined to find that out.

Chapter Three

"So, if you just rewrite the conclusion, you'll be set." Erin glanced at her watch and exhaled. "That's it. And don't forget to study the flashcards. You'll need to know those dates for the test." She gathered the scattered papers and notecards and passed them to the student seated across the kitchen table.

"Thanks, Ms. McCuen." Morgan Butler scooped up the stack of papers and smiled, her braces glinting in the overhead light.

Erin rose and glanced out the dark kitchen window, then forced her gaze away. She had to stop watching for Wade. So what if he hadn't returned by dinner—or several hours after? He didn't have to apprise her of every move. But according to Lottie, Norm's condition had worsened that morning, and she couldn't help but worry.

She followed Morgan down the hall to the foyer where the girl put on her coat. As she waited, she caught the distant pulse of a Harley. Her heart paused, then thrummed with expectation. Wade was back. She hoped that meant good news.

The throaty vibrations grew louder. She turned and pressed her forehead to the window. A moment later Wade's headlight flashed and bobbed up the drive.

"Are you tutoring somebody else tonight?" Morgan asked.

"No, it's just my renter." The teen picked up her papers from the hutch and joined her at the window. The bike passed the porch and the engine abruptly cut off.

Suddenly in a rush to dispatch Morgan, she hurried the girl out the door. "See you tomorrow," she called as Morgan descended the steps. "And drive carefully."

Wade stomped up the porch seconds later. She moved back to let him inside and closed the door against the chill.

He paused under the chandelier and her gaze flew to his eyes. His bloodshot eyes. Down to the stark lines bracketing his mouth and the haggard cast to his features.

Her stomach swooped. "Oh, no. Did Norm—?"

"Yeah." He turned and limped to the stairs. He climbed slowly, stiffly, his boots heavy on the creaking steps. At the landing, he crossed to the bedroom and slammed the door.

A deep ache lodged in her chest. Dear Norm. He'd been the nicest man. He'd adopted a boy no one had wanted. He'd used his savings to pay her grandmother's bills. He'd dedicated his life to helping their tiny town. Why did someone that kind have to die?

Her eyes burned, but she willed back the hot rush of tears. Her grandmother had gone to bed early, so she'd tell her the news in the morning. But she should call Lottie—and Max to see if he needed help. And bake a coffee cake for the neighbors who'd gather at the duplex tomorrow.

But more importantly, she had to help Wade. Her gaze traveled up the stairs. Norm meant everything to him. How on earth would he cope?

She walked across the foyer to the staircase, then paused with her hand on the newel post. Wade hadn't asked for her sympathy. He hadn't even lingered to talk. He'd gone straight to his room and shut the door, isolating himself, just as he had as a kid.

Maybe she should give him some space. He obviously wanted his privacy, and he really was none of her business. But how could she leave him alone at a time like this?

And that was exactly how he'd feel right now— alone. He'd just lost his entire family. The one person in the world who cared.

Or so he thought. She cared, and always had. Enough to go to him now, even if he only rebuffed her.

Her feet heavy, she climbed the stairs. He didn't answer her knock, which didn't really surprise her. She tapped again, waited, then cautiously inched open the door. "Wade?"

Light spilled from the hallway into the darkened room. He stood with his arms crossed, facing the window, staring out at the night. He looked vulnerable standing there alone. Lonely. Desolation wedged hard in her throat.

He didn't glance at her as she crossed the room or when she placed her hand on his arm. He didn't even acknowledge her presence. But neither did he pull away.

Relieved, she hitched out her breath, then stood beside him in the darkness. She inhaled the scent of his leather jacket, along with a faint trace of whiskey. Her heart twisted. How typical of Wade to exile himself to a bar and deal with his pain alone. He never did believe anyone cared.

But Norm had cared, and Wade needed to remember that. "You know he thought of you as his son," she said.

He tensed, but she kept her hand on his arm. "He saved every letter you wrote. He read them to us all the time—at the café, the grocery store, whenever we stopped by the house... We heard about your years on the hotshot crews, your rookie training. And when you made smokejumper, I'd never seen anyone so proud."

She smiled at the memory. "He carried around a photo of you in your jump gear. He showed it to us dozens of times. It got so worn out you could hardly tell who it was anymore, but his face still lit up when he pulled it out."

She heard him suck in his breath, felt his arm tremble beneath her palm. Tears thickened her throat, but she forced herself to go on. "We heard about every jump you ever made. And we're experts on smoke-jumping now, thanks to Norm. You could give us a quiz—sticks and stobs, speed racks, streamers. He hardly talked about anything else.

"And that video you sent him...he watched it over

and over…" Her voice broke on a sob. "He loved you so much, Wade, and he was so proud of how you turned out. You need to remember that."

Wade covered his eyes with his hand. And suddenly she couldn't bear it. Her own eyes burning, she stepped behind him and wrapped her arms around his waist. Unable to speak, she pressed her cheek to his back and held tight.

He stood stiffly as she hugged him and she thought he might jerk away. But after several tense seconds, he eased back and she shut her eyes in relief.

She wasn't offering him much, just human touch and kindness. But then, she never had given him what he needed. She'd tried, Lord, how she'd tried, but he'd always pushed her away.

Except that night at the river, when he'd finally lowered his guard. The time he'd shared his heart, along with his body. But afterward, he'd built up his walls again and pretended it had only been sex. But it had been love—deep, soul-baring love, at least for her. And she would have sworn he'd felt the same.

The minutes stretched in thick silence. Then, without warning, she felt the muscles of his back flex and his tension rise again.

"He had a damn DNR in place," he said suddenly, his deep voice rough with anger. "An order not to resuscitate. Hell. I had to sit there and let him die."

She tightened her grip, sensing the horror, the pain he'd endured. Wade lived in constant action—flinging himself into the slipstream, leaping into forests to battle fires. Sitting by helplessly while Norm died would have driven him out of his mind.

But Norm had made that decision and there'd been nothing Wade could do. "He'd been in a lot of pain," she said. "He probably felt it was time to go."

Wade retreated into silence. Minutes lengthened, along with the shadows in the room. Finally she heard him exhale. He understood, but needed time to process the grief.

And she'd done all she could. She eased her hold and stepped back. He turned to face her and she saw the despair in his eyes.

Sorrow clawed at her chest. She wanted so badly to take care of this man, to erase the grief from his heart. She'd give anything to have that right.

But she didn't. She was just an old friend. She stepped even farther away. "Are you hungry?"

"No." His voice was gruff and threaded with sadness. "But thanks."

He peeled off his jacket and tossed it on the wing chair near the dresser, then sat on the bed and removed his boots. When he dropped back on the bedspread and threw his arm over his eyes, she knew she ought to go.

But she couldn't bear to leave him yet. Her chest full, she picked up the lap quilt from the wing chair and spread it over his legs. Then she perched beside him on the bed and cradled his free hand in hers.

What more could she say? What could ease the pain of losing a father? She shook her head, knowing it was futile to try.

So she just sat there and held his hand until his breathing deepened and slowed. Until his grip slackened and she knew he slept in the darkness. She stroked the scars along the back of his hand, the calluses on his palm, felt the strength and power in his fingers.

And remembered other stories Norm had told her, of the terrible risks Wade had taken. How he'd jumped the most volatile fires and worked in the steepest terrain. Because he believed he was expendable. That no one would miss him if he died. That no one cared.

But he'd been wrong.

His arm fell back against the pillow and she gazed at his hard, shadowed face. Her chest tightened and swelled with longing. She'd loved this man her entire life. He'd been everything to her, from a childhood hero and teenage crush, to the man she'd yearned to marry.

She'd given him her virginity, along with her heart. She would have given anything if he'd loved her back, if they could have spent their lives together.

But he hadn't, and she'd shelved those hopes long ago.

But not the memories.

Her gaze traced a path down the rugged planes of his face, and she dragged in a shaky breath. Maybe it was the moonlight, the way the smoky beams cast shadows over his face. Or maybe she was simply too drained, too weary to fend off the emotions tonight. But she couldn't stop the images from flooding back, the wild need swamping her heart.

It had been hot, so hot, and the soft rush of the river, the languid buzz of insects permeated the night. She'd stood beside him on the wooded towpath, gazing out at the swirling water, far from the party downstream. The sultry heat slugged through her blood. Moisture beaded her skin.

And an awful weight pressed on her chest, blocking out everything except that one thought. That he was leaving in the morning. That she might never see him again.

That she only had this one chance, this last night, to do what she'd always dreamed.

She'd turned to him then. The moonlight teased the angles of his masculine face, shrouding his dark eyes in shadow. She dragged at the sweltering air. The buzz of the insects grew louder.

And she moved deliberately closer.

He stilled and his dark gaze locked on hers. Neither spoke. The damp woods rustled around them. Tension pulsed through the air.

She knew she was crossing a line, an unspoken boundary between them, but she'd wanted him, fantasized about him for so long. And sometimes, when those whiskey-brown eyes seared hers, she'd suspected he wanted her, too. But he'd always kept his distance and she'd never had the nerve.

Until now.

Now she had this one night to make those fantasies come true.

Hardly breathing, she reached up and ran her hand across his bristled jaw. His rough skin burned beneath her palm; the erotic texture thrilled her.

But he grabbed her wrist and blocked her. "Erin," he warned, his deep voice flat.

She nearly lost her nerve then, and she flushed. But the heat in his eyes gave her courage. She sensed that he wanted this, wanted her, but wouldn't let himself touch her. That somehow, in his need to protect her, he'd placed her firmly off limits.

Her heart stuttering hard against her rib cage, she shook off his hand and inched closer. Much closer, until her breasts skimmed his chest and his ragged breath heated her face.

"Wade," she whispered. "Kiss me."

His jaw turned rigid. His fierce gaze burned into hers.

"Please," she whispered again, her urgency rising. She couldn't bear it if he turned away.

"Erin…" His voice sounded strangled, tortured.

"Just a kiss. Just…" His gaze scorched her lips. Cicadas screamed in the air.

Then he lifted his hands and her breath stalled. And he blazed a trail along her jaw, stroking her neck, her throat with his thumbs, sending ripples of excitement splintering through her.

The air around them stilled. Her pulse ran wild in her throat. And then he tugged up her chin and angled his head, and moved his mouth over hers. Slowly, tenderly. As if she were something fragile, something precious.

As if he loved her.

Her lungs seized up. Her eyes fluttered closed and her heart refused to beat.

But then he probed the seam of her mouth with his tongue and she parted her lips on a gasp. And his tongue swept through her mouth, bold and sure, and insistent, until shivers blazed over her skin and hot blood pooled in her veins.

He widened his stance and pulled her against his arousal. The sensation shocked her. Excited her. Her heart nearly leaped from her chest.

And then he groaned and tightened his arms, and seemed to lose all control, devouring her in a deep, carnal kiss that blasted away every thought. Jolting her, flaying her, reeling her in deeper and harder. Until a fever of need scorched her nerves and her body quivered with pleasure.

She moaned against his mouth, feeling dazed, drugged, obsessed. She craved his big, rough hands on her skin. His hard body fused with hers.

But he pushed her head to his neck and clamped her tightly against him. Her heart thundered inside her chest. His breath rasped loud in her ear.

"Wade, make love to me," she whimpered.

"No, Erin." His voice was jagged, hoarse. "Don't do this."

"Please." Desperate, she pressed herself against him. She'd die if he left her now.

"You don't know what you're asking." He was trembling, sucking in air, as if he'd run ten miles.

"Yes, I do. I want you."

She pulled her head from his grasp. His eyes were stark. Emotions warred in his face. Resistance. Frustration. Hunger.

"Wade, please," she pleaded, her voice breaking.

"I'll hurt you. Don't you understand? I don't want to hurt you."

"You won't. You can't." She burned for him, ached for him to fill that void inside her. "I need you."

He tipped back his head and shuddered. He made a deep, rough sound in his throat.

And then he hauled her against him and crushed his mouth over hers, ravaging her, scalding her, until need overcame thought. Until their senses burned and their bodies merged, and she knew what it meant to love.

It had been exquisite, the most thrilling night of her life. A perfect moment in time.

But reality returned with the dawn and he'd closed down that glimpse of his heart. And she'd realized that it hadn't been enough, that she couldn't convince him to stay. And she'd stood there alone on her porch, her heart shattering, her entire world collapsing, as the Harley's rumble receded and the man she loved rode away.

Her deep sigh cut through the night. And now he was back in her life. Not by choice, of course. And nothing had really changed. He didn't want a relationship. And he certainly didn't want her love. All she could offer was friendship, for however long he stayed—which wouldn't be long now that Norm had died.

She sighed again, heavier this time. She didn't envy him the days ahead. Attending the funeral. Settling the estate. Dispensing with Norm's belongings.

Then another thought occurred to her and a dull dread crept through her heart. With Norm gone, she had to repay the loan. Norm had never pressed her for payments, but now she didn't have a choice.

But where could she get the money? She'd already taken out one bank loan and she had nowhere else to turn.

She also had to tell Wade. He would probably inherit Norm's estate, so she'd owe him the money now.

She frowned at that complication. Wade had enough

to contend with without burdening him with her problems. But she could hardly avoid telling him. She'd do it the first chance she had.

Uneasy now, she gently released his hand. She tucked the quilt around his legs, then rose, hoping in sleep he'd find the peace he deserved. A peace that would elude her until she found a way to repay Norm's loan.

Chapter Four

Cars and trucks lined Norm's street when Wade pulled up the next morning. He took one glance at the throng of vehicles and nearly kept on going.

But he'd already ridden for hours and it hadn't done any good. After a miserable, restless night, he'd dragged himself out of bed, jumped on his Harley, and hurtled down the country roads—just opened the throttle and unleashed the V-Rod's raw power. But the grief still clamped down on him, crushing him, like a huge vise squeezing his chest.

And the last thing he wanted to do right now was to deal with people. He didn't want condolences and he sure as hell didn't want pity. But he couldn't leave town yet. He'd promised Norm he'd stay and he would, until they buried him in the ground.

A sharp ache knifed through his chest, but he sucked

in a ragged breath. Then, before he could change his mind, he parked the bike, strode up the short cement walkway and pushed open the door to the kitchen.

As he'd expected, the house overflowed with neighbors. Max waved from across the kitchen to get his attention, and worked his way to him through the crowd.

"Wade, thank God you're here." Max clapped his hand on his shoulder. "Ed from the funeral parlor called. You need to call him back."

Wade spotted the coffee machine on the counter, flanked by cakes and rolls. "Why does he want to talk to me?"

"He needs to know what you decided about the funeral."

"What do you mean, what I decided? Why couldn't you handle that?" He moved to the counter, tugged a foam cup off the stack and poured himself some coffee.

"Because you're next of kin. And I wasn't sure if you'd want a viewing or just the service."

Viewing? Service? What the hell did he care? He wanted to bury Norm and leave town.

"They'll send the obituary to the newspaper, too," Max added. "As soon as you confirm the details. Norm left everything you'd need with the will."

"Everything I'd need for what? What are you talking about?"

Max scratched his head. "You didn't know? Norm told me it was all set."

He slugged back the coffee, then narrowed his eyes at Max. "Exactly what am I supposed to know?"

"That you're executor of the will."

"Executor? You're kidding." How could he do that? Didn't an executor have to file papers? Pay taxes? Jump through hoops of red tape? "I don't even live here anymore."

Max shrugged. "It shouldn't take long. A few months maybe."

"A few months!"

"Maybe longer. They can tell you at the courthouse."

He stared at Max. He couldn't stay here for months; he could barely tolerate days. And Norm knew that. So why had he saddled him with this job?

Because he knew Wade wouldn't turn him down— which meant he'd wanted him to stay. But why?

He scowled. Norm had never asked him to live in Millstown, never even brought that subject up. Besides, what would Wade do in Millstown with Norm gone?

An image of Erin's sagging porch came to mind. Hell. Was that what this was about?

Anger flared, then slammed through his gut. Did Erin know about this arrangement? Had she schemed with Norm behind his back? Just what the hell was she up to?

He thought of her sweet body pressed to his back, her gentle voice in the dark, and his fury abruptly deflated. No, Erin hadn't done this. She would never manipulate him that way. Norm had hatched this plot alone.

But that still didn't mean that he liked it.

The phone trilled across the noisy room. "Hey, Wade," someone called a moment later. "It's Ed from the funeral home again."

Still seething, he dumped his remaining coffee in the

sink and slammed the cup in the trash. He'd deal with the funeral parlor. And the paper. And the courthouse, and anything else that he had to.

He'd been boned from the bottom. He didn't have a choice.

But damned if he would stay in Millstown one minute longer than it took to settle that will. Not one second longer. No matter what Norm had in mind.

Early that evening, with both his knee and skull now hammering, Wade returned to Mills Ferry. He hauled himself up the stairs, intending to gulp down some painkillers and crash into bed.

"Do you have a minute, Wade?"

He stopped partway up the stairs and looked down. Erin stood in the foyer, her red hair shimmering in the light. She clasped her hands together. "I need to talk to you, if you don't mind."

"Sure." He trudged back down the stairs. She probably wanted to talk about Norm. He hoped she cut it short. He didn't want to chat after making funeral arrangements all day.

"Grandma's watching TV in the parlor, so why don't we talk in the kitchen?"

"Fine." He glanced into the small front room as he passed. The older woman sat in an armchair, wrapped in a colorful quilt.

He limped behind Erin toward the kitchen. Despite the pain ramming his skull, he appreciated the view. Her tight, faded jeans hugged her lushly curved bottom and highlighted the flare of her hips.

Then she leaned against the kitchen counter and

crossed her arms, and his gaze lodged on her breasts, just as it always had in high school. The corner of his mouth kicked up. She'd driven him crazy back then. He'd spent years in a haze of lust, imagining how she'd look and feel naked.

But no fantasy had matched the reality of Erin. The taste of her delicate skin. The satiny feel of her breasts. And when he'd been inside her...

He shifted, swallowed hard. "Dinner smells good."

She flashed a nervous smile. "I made chicken enchiladas. I hope you like Mexican food."

"I like anything I can eat."

"It's nothing fancy. I'm not that great a cook."

Why did she need to apologize? "Believe me, I'm not picky. I'm a smokejumper, remember?"

"What does that have to do with it?"

"Constant hunger. Even ratted C-rations look good after a few days working a fire." He tugged the waistband of his jeans, which had ridden low on his hips. "You can't eat enough to keep the weight on. That's why my jeans are so loose."

Her gaze skimmed down his chest to his waist. And then lower. Her cheeks flushed and hot desire lashed his groin.

Thrown off guard, he pulled out a chair and sat. The abrupt movement jolted his knee but he welcomed the distraction. "So what did you want to talk about?"

Her forehead furrowed. "There's something you need to know. Norm lent me some money a while back. Quite a bit, actually. Ten thousand dollars.

"Grandma's accident generated a lot of bills," she continued. "Medicare covered most of them, but she doesn't have a supplement, so the extras added up. The drugs alone cost a fortune. And then there's this house." She sighed. "I love it, but it's an absolute money pit. Everything's breaking and rotting away. And then the roof started leaking and I had to have it repaired. It really needs to be replaced, but—"

"Erin, why are you telling me this?"

She sighed, more heavily this time. "Because I can't pay it back. Not yet, anyway. I will, but I—"

"Forget it."

"What?"

"I said forget it. Norm's dead. He doesn't need the money."

"But—"

"Look, I read the will today and he left almost everything to me. And I don't want the money." Or the delay collecting the debt would cause. He stood.

"Wade, did you hear me? I said I owe you ten thousand dollars."

"And I said I don't need it."

"But everybody needs—"

"Listen. I make good money at what I do, and I rake in the overtime pay." He shrugged. "And I don't have many expenses. Maybe I'm not rich by some standards, but I'm sure as hell not poor."

She shook her head. "Even if I wanted to let you forget it—and I certainly don't—you might not have a choice. I don't know much about settling estates, but I don't think you can just write off a debt like that."

"So I'll take the money out of my account and put it into Norm's. What difference does it make?"

"It makes a difference to me."

"Erin, Norm gave the money to you."

"He *lent* the money to me. There's a difference."

"Well, I don't want the money, so just forget it." He started toward the door.

"Oh, no, you don't." She stalked into his path and put out her hand to block him. "Stop right there! Just stop! You are *not* going to do this. I absolutely won't let you."

He frowned down at her. "Not do what?"

"Riding in here like some knight in shining armor, throwing your money around to solve my problems, and then bolting away again."

Her green eyes blazed at him. She was actually angry. Because he didn't want her money? Or because he was going to leave?

Dread spiraled through his gut. "This is about that night at the river, isn't it?"

"What?" she gasped.

"You're mad because I left."

"I am not!"

He plunged his hand through his hair. "Erin, I couldn't stay in Millstown."

"And I never asked you to." She planted her hands on her hips. "I knew all along you were leaving. You'd talked about it for months. So don't you dare put that guilt on yourself. Don't you dare! I knew exactly what I was doing."

She sure did. She'd excited him out of his mind and he'd fantasized about it ever since.

Color rode high on her cheeks. "I was the one who suggested it, if you recall. And I got what I wanted."

"What? A night of sex?"

"That's right."

His own temper flared. It had been a hell of a lot more than that and she knew it.

And it had scared him to death.

He stilled. Is that why he'd rushed off? Because he couldn't deal with his feelings for Erin? Or had he been protecting her from himself, as he'd convinced himself all these years?

He'd been a rough, scrappy kid from the trailer trash side of town, not the kind of man she should marry. He'd had no skills, no way to earn a living. Of course he'd been right to leave.

The telephone rang in the tense silence. A second later it rang again. He motioned toward it with his hand. "Aren't you going to get that?"

"The machine can pick it up."

The phone rang again and the answering machine beeped on. "Erin, this is Mike," the machine recorded. "I wanted to know if you'd like to go to the symphony tomorrow night. I've got the bank's box, if you're interested. I thought we could have dinner first, maybe around seven?"

Erin lifted a shoulder, her face still flushed. "Mike Kell," she explained. "He teaches with me at St. Michaels."

Mike Kell. Sure, he remembered. Class president and valedictorian. His father owned the bank. Wade's jaw clenched.

"…so give me a call when you get in," Mike finished. The machine clicked off, paused, then whirred as it rewound.

"I take it you're dating?"

"Not really."

He scowled. "Dinner and the symphony sounds like a date to me."

"We're just friends."

But Mike wanted it to be more, he guessed. And Mike was exactly the type Erin belonged with. Classy, educated. Irritation surged in his gut.

His gaze settled on the shadows under her eyes, the fatigue lining her face, and his temper rose. So why wasn't Mike taking care of her? He wouldn't let her suffer if she belonged to him—teaching rowdy kids all day, slaving over her grandmother at night, scraping by on borrowed money while her house rotted apart. Why didn't Mike grab a chain saw and cut up those limbs in the yard or pick up a hammer and fix the porch?

Erin's gaze caught his. "Look, I'm going to pay back the money. I just need time to organize things, that's all."

"And I said I don't want it."

Her chin came up. "Well, that's too bad because I'm still going to pay it back. This isn't your problem."

"Norm made it my problem."

She crossed her arms, her pride apparent in the tilt of her head. But another emotion flitted through her eyes. Worry. Anxiety. And suddenly she looked vulnerable, lost, like that abandoned kid she'd once been.

The kid with rejection haunting her eyes from a mother who didn't want her. The kid who'd flashed him that sweet, shy smile, despite his bad reputation. The one who had accepted him.

A hard fist twisted his heart. He didn't mean to trample her pride, and he sure didn't want to hurt her. He never could stand to wound Erin.

But she obviously couldn't solve this alone. Even if she paid off the loan, the house still needed attention. And who knew what other debts she had, or what she'd do in the future?

Which meant he had to get involved, whether she liked it or not. She had no one else to help her.

"You don't mind if I stay here, do you?" he asked slowly. "While I'm going through Norm's things, I mean."

"Of course not. You can stay as long as you want."

"Good." That would give him time to fix the house and solve the rest of her problems. He turned and strode toward the door.

"Wade."

He paused and turned back. Her green eyes narrowed on his. "I'm serious. I said I don't want a savior."

But she sure as hell needed one. And it appeared it was going to be him.

Chapter Five

The early morning sunlight filtered through the third-story window, casting weak, dust-laden rays across the room. Wade clicked on his flashlight and aimed the beam at the sagging ceiling. Pooling water had stained and damaged the plaster and buckled the wood floor beneath.

Disgusted, he turned off the flashlight and crossed to the deep-set window. The old bubbled glass was still intact, but the wooden sill had rotted, letting cold wind whistle through. He shook his head. No wonder the house was freezing. Every window in the whole damned place leaked.

He propped the flashlight on the sill, tugged his notepad from his back pocket and added to his growing list. The house was in far worse shape than he'd expected. Chimneys had cracked. The exterior stone needed repointing. The foundation had settled, causing the ground floor to warp.

And the interior was even worse. He could paint, plaster, sand and refinish every day for the rest of his life and never run out of work. And he hadn't even looked at the heating or plumbing.

He braced his hand on the window frame and scowled out at a sprawling oak tree. So much for repairing Erin's house while he settled Norm's estate. No way could he finish these jobs in the short time he'd be here.

So what could he do? Erin couldn't afford to hire out the work, and she would refuse to let him pay. But he couldn't leave Millstown with her house in this condition.

He straightened. There was only one solution and Erin wasn't going to like it. She had to sell Mills Ferry.

"So here you are," she said from behind him. "I wondered where you'd run off to. Max called to see if you have time to sort through some boxes."

He turned as she crossed the room. His gaze swept her high, full breasts, down the length of her shapely thighs, then jerked back up to her eyes. Her gentle, knowing eyes.

His heart rolled in his chest. She had the damnedest effect on him, making him want to ravish and protect her.

She stopped beside him. "So what are you doing up here, anyway?"

He eyed the fiery hair smoldering in the soft morning light, the familiar set to her jaw, and knew that she would resist this. "I thought I'd check out the house, see about fixing some things while I'm here."

Her eyes narrowed. "Wade, I told you—"

"Yeah, I know. That you don't need my help. But I'll be bored just sitting around filing papers. Besides, I'm good with my hands."

Her cheeks flushed and she looked away. The memory slammed into him again, that vision of his hands sliding over her bare, ripe breasts, her naked skin shimmering pale in the moonlight.

He forced himself to breathe. "I just want to help, okay?"

She looked back at him and a frown creased her forehead, her practicality warring with pride. After a moment she sighed. "Fine. Feel free to hammer away. Lord knows the place needs work."

Did she have any idea how much? He rubbed the back of his neck. He wanted to repair her beloved house and make her happy, but as every smokejumper knew, you couldn't catch every fire. Sometimes you just had to let one burn. And it wasn't practical to fix Mills Ferry.

"It needs more work than I expected," he admitted. "And it's going to be expensive. Have you considered selling the place?"

"Selling it?" Her soft mouth sagged. "Oh, I could never do that. It's been in my family for ten generations. It was on the Underground Railroad, you know."

"And it was a hospital in the Civil War, and there are bloodstains on the floors to prove it. You gave me that tour in fourth grade."

The edges of her lips curled up. "That day was the highlight of my life until then. I couldn't believe everyone wanted to see my house. It was the first time I felt important."

"Yeah." It had been the highlight of his life, too. The two motherless kids had forged a bond that day that had endured for years.

Of course, Erin had a mother back then; she'd just cared more about her jet-setting lifestyle than making a home for her daughter. She'd dumped Erin off in Millstown so she could flit around the globe.

Erin leaned against the wall. "I was stunned when my mom dropped me off here. After all those years of traipsing around the world, getting pawned off on strangers, I suddenly had a home, a history, a place where I really belonged."

Her eyes met his. "I'd feel like a failure if I had to sell. My family's kept this house through all sorts of disasters—the Civil War, the Depression… I'd feel awful if I lost it now. Besides, I love this house. I don't want to live anywhere else."

The place had character, all right. It had fascinated him as a kid—the slave quarters under the house, the ruined mill along the river, the bunkers from the Civil War…

But it was the turret off the third floor that really fired his imagination. He still remembered when Erin had grabbed his hand and led him to the top. He didn't know which had impressed him more: the fairy-tale house or the princess who'd chosen him for her friend.

"It's a great house," he agreed. "But it needs a lot of work."

"I know the roof still leaks."

"The roof is just the start. We're talking major repairs here. Foundation joists. Sagging floors."

"Is it really that bad?" Her exquisite green eyes searched his.

He handed her the list he'd compiled.

Her forehead creased as she studied it, then she turned her gaze to the window. After a moment her shoulders slumped.

She looked defeated suddenly, vulnerable, and he wished that he could protect her. He wanted to kiss the worry from her wrinkled brow and shelter her from the harsh side of life. But this was her house and she had to know the truth.

His gaze roamed the smattering of freckles across her nose and the soft, lush curve of her lips. Then she shivered in the unheated air, and his gaze dropped to her breasts.

His body instantly hardened, which came as no surprise. He'd responded to Erin for years. And not just physically. Even when they were kids, he couldn't resist her. He'd do anything to make her happy.

He'd sure as hell tried. He'd given her the night she'd wanted, then left so she could find the man she deserved.

She handed him back the list with a sigh. "It looks like a mess, all right, but I'll figure something out."

"What's there to figure out? You have to sell."

"And I told you I can't do that."

He jammed the notepad into his back pocket. "I know you don't want to, but—"

"I can't. So let's just drop it, okay?"

"Drop what? Erin, you have to face facts. This place is falling apart."

"And I said I don't care."

"But—"

"I'm not keeping it just for my sake. Oh, I love this

place, and it'll kill me to let it go. But I can't sell now, not while Grandma's alive. I owe her everything for taking me in. And I could never put her out of her house."

He tried for a reasonable tone. "I'm not saying you should dump her on the street. But you could buy a condo, or maybe put her in a nursing home. It would be cheaper than maintaining this place."

She shook her head. "I tried that. Well, not a nursing home exactly, but a day-care place for the elderly. It was after she got out of the hospital and I had to go back to work.

"It was awful. She didn't understand where she was or why she had to go there. She cried when I dropped her off. And when we came home at night, she just sat in the sunroom for hours, rocking and clutching her quilts.

"She couldn't cope with the change. Maybe because she's always lived here, but mostly because of the accident. She doesn't remember much anymore."

She let out a heavy sigh. "Thank goodness for Lottie. I was so lucky to get her. I don't know what I'd do if she left."

Frustration knotted his gut. He understood her problem, but where did that leave her? Living in debt, in a dilapidated house, taking care of two old ladies?

That was typical of Erin, always helping everyone else. But who took care of her?

She shivered again and goose bumps rose on her arms. He jerked off his sweatshirt. "Here. Put this on."

"Oh, no. Thanks, but—"

"For God's sake. Put it on." He pulled it over her

head. Her hair caught under the sweatshirt and a few short wisps floated loose.

"But, Wade, I—"

"Just stick your damned hands through." Did she have to argue everything? Couldn't she let him help her for once?

She pushed her hands through the sleeves, then reached back to free her hair as he tugged the sweatshirt over her chest. His hands grazed her breasts and he heard her suck in her breath.

Their eyes locked and for several heartbeats neither moved. Tension drummed between them. The blood pulsed hard in his ears.

He dropped his gaze to her lips, her soft, full lips, and suddenly he wanted to kiss her. To weigh her breasts in his palms again, to feel her silky skin.

But he didn't have that right. She didn't belong to him and never would.

But was it wrong to seek her warmth, even just for a moment?

Reaching up, he traced the curve of her cheek with his hand and stroked the tender slope of her neck. Her eyes darkened and he swallowed hard. Surely one kiss couldn't hurt.

He angled his head as her lashes closed, and brushed his lips across hers. She was so gentle, so sweet. When her arms tightened around his neck, he instinctively gathered her closer.

He traced the seam of her mouth with his tongue and entered when her moist lips parted. He felt her welcome, her acceptance. Desire surged with an intensity that shocked him.

But this was wrong. He shouldn't touch her. He forced himself to pull back.

His breathing rasped loud in the silence. He knew he should drop his hands, step away. Stop clutching her hair and breathing her warm, sweet scent. Stop feeling her full breasts brushing his chest and her hips cradling his growing arousal.

But then she stroked his neck, sending pleasure shocking along his skin, and he found it hard to think.

"Wade," she whispered with her siren's voice. "Kiss me again."

And he was lost. He couldn't deny Erin, couldn't resist her gentle plea.

With a groan, he lowered his head and gave in to his mounting hunger. He kissed her thoroughly this time, lengthening and deepening the kiss. Delving her warm, soft depths and losing himself to sensation. Exactly the way he'd longed to, the way he'd dreamed.

After an eternity he broke away. His heart rocketing, his blood slamming through his veins, he rained kisses along her neck and tasted the seductive heat of her skin.

"Wade," she gasped, and the soft sound tore at his heart.

And his crumbling resistance shattered. He kissed her again, feverishly, while stark need clawed at his chest. Longing consumed him, a fierce and desperate yearning. A need only she could ease.

She was his home. Where he belonged. And God, it had been so long.

With hunger pounding his brain, he moved even closer and fitted himself to her warmth. A moan escaped her and he shuddered, knowing he was losing control.

And he finally answered the question that had plagued him for years. Teenage hormones hadn't made that night fantastic; it had been Erin. Only Erin. He couldn't delude himself ever again.

With hot need knotting his gut, he raised his head and looked around. He eyed the floor, the wall.

But this was Erin. He couldn't treat her like that. But damned if he wasn't tempted.

That thought stopped him cold. She wasn't the type for casual sex. Hell, she wasn't the type for him.

He was wrong for her and always had been. He couldn't give her what she needed or what she deserved—a decent, settled man who'd stay in Millstown and raise a family.

He pulled her arms from his neck. "Erin," he rasped. She opened her eyes, looking dazed. Her hair was mussed, her lips swollen. He wanted to yank her close and kiss her senseless.

"I'm sorry. I... That got out of hand." The confusion in her eyes turned to frustration and he felt his stomach clench. He wanted her more than he wanted to breathe; she had to realize that. But he couldn't hurt her that way. He had to protect her, even from himself.

He forced himself to step back. "I shouldn't have let it go that far, but it... God, I'm sorry, I..."

Just then something vibrated against his thigh. Startled, he tore his gaze from Erin and glanced down. His beeper-alarm was buzzing. He fumbled in his pocket and pulled it out, then frowned at the display.

It took several seconds for the message to register.

Full alert. Someone was leaning his bike upright. Someone was trying to start it?

"What is it?" she asked, her voice husky.

"I'm not sure." Still struggling to clear his head, he strode to the window and peered out. Someone sat astride his Harley in the driveway, tinkering with the controls. He frowned. "Some kid's stealing my bike."

At least he was trying to. The security system disabled the starter, so he doubted the kid could succeed. Still, he wasn't going to let him try.

He turned back to Erin. "Look, I'm sorry, I...I'll be back."

He pulled his gaze from her and bolted from the room. Then he raced down the two flights of stairs, ran out the door and jumped down the front porch steps. The landing jolted his knee and he swore.

The kid looked up as Wade rounded the house, his footsteps pounding the gravel. He leaped off the bike and fled toward the nearby woods.

Wade chased him, his temper rising. The kid was skinny, in his early teens, and fast. But despite his injured knee, Wade was in top condition.

He caught up with him at the wall. The kid had one leg over the top, but Wade grabbed his sweatshirt and yanked him back. They both fell in a pile of dry leaves. The kid leaped up swinging, but Wade crouched and knocked him down.

Breathing hard, he angled his body over the kid to subdue him and clenched his shirt at the neck. The teen's eyes bugged wide, then narrowed in a show of bravado.

For several minutes neither spoke. Sweat trickled

down Wade's cheek. A cardinal whistled in the silence. He loosened his grip to give the kid air, but wasn't fooled when he stopped struggling.

"All right," he said, still panting. "I'm letting you up now. Don't even think of running away."

He let go and got to his feet. The teen rose more slowly, then suddenly lunged for freedom, just as Wade had expected.

Wade went for his knees. He tackled the kid to the ground and in one sharp movement twisted his arm up his back. Then, with his knee planted on the boy's spine, he rammed his face to the ground.

He held him longer this time, so the kid could consider his options. "You ready to listen?" he finally asked.

"Yeah." The kid's voice was muffled by leaves.

"I mean it," he warned. "You run again and I'll break your arm." He wrenched it higher for emphasis.

"I'll stay!"

He waited several more seconds, then slowly released him and stood. The teen got to his feet, massaged his arm and pulled the leaves from his sweatshirt. He shot Wade a sullen look.

Wade surveyed the kid's baggy pants and earrings, the blond fuzz on his smooth jaw, and inwardly sighed. Damn, the kid looked young. Or was he just getting old? "What's your name?"

"Sean. Gill," he added when Wade lifted his brows.

"So, Sean Gill. I take it you like my bike?"

"Yeah, so what?"

"So no one touches it without my permission. And I get ticked when someone tries to steal it."

"You can't prove that."

He crossed his arms and studied the kid. A faded bruise marred his cheek and he had a hard edge to his eyes, as if he'd already been through the system. As Wade had at that age.

"Oh, I can prove it," he said flatly. "I saw you, and so did the McCuens." He jerked his head toward the house. "And you can bet the police will believe them."

Panic sparked in his eyes, but he gave a show of indifference. "So go ahead and report me. I don't care."

Wade was tempted. It would be easier to let the police handle this. And he sure as hell didn't need another problem. But something about the kid tugged at him, stirring his conscience, reminding him of himself.

He dragged in a breath and let it out. Felt a dull throb slide through his skull. Damn, but he didn't need this.

But he knew that the system wouldn't save this kid. The arrest wouldn't scare him; he was already too jaded. And another stint at juvenile hall would only harden him more.

Which meant that if he wanted to help this kid, he had to do it himself.

Just as Norm had taught him. The corner of his mouth kicked up. Norm would have appreciated that irony.

"Okay," he said. "Here's the deal. I'll forget this episode under one condition. You work for me for a while, help me clean this place up, and I won't call the police."

"And if I don't want to?"

Wade stared at him hard. The kid met his gaze for several seconds, then shifted his feet and looked down.

"Be here tomorrow at three. And come prepared to work."

That settled, he turned and strode toward the house. He paused to check that his bike was intact, but didn't glance back at the kid. He'd probably scaled the wall and run off. But he'd be back.

Erin opened the door to the sun porch. "That's Sean Gill," she said. She handed him the flashlight he'd left upstairs. "He lives in Newburg Village. I subbed in one of his classes before I got hired at St. Michaels."

Newburg Village. The same trailer park he'd lived in.

"We think his father beats him, but no one's been able to prove it. Both Sean and his mother deny it. It's a sad situation."

Sad was right. Just as his own childhood had been. He tapped the flashlight against his palm. "Yeah, well, he's coming by tomorrow to do some work."

"Tomorrow?" A small line creased her forehead. "But people are stopping by after the funeral. I hope you don't mind. It's a potluck type of thing."

"No, I don't mind." Although he wished she hadn't bothered. She didn't need to fuss over him. "The kid's coming at three. Won't they be gone by then?"

"I suppose."

He gazed into her hypnotic eyes, aware that he hadn't made much progress. He would repair what he could around the place, maybe even convince her to forget the loan. But that was just a temporary solution, like knocking down flare-ups or spot fires. How could he solve her problems long-term if she refused to sell?

"I'd better get over to Norm's," he said. "And help Max with those boxes." He stepped back and turned away.

But one thing was certain, he thought as he limped back through the house. Erin didn't need him complicating her life. Which meant that from now on, no matter how badly he wanted to touch her, he had to keep his hands to himself.

Chapter Six

Everyone always died in the winter. His mother, Rose, Norm...Wade stood before the newly dug grave, the raw wind blasting his face. His vision blurred as he watched the bare trees at the edge of the cemetery claw at the tombstone-hued sky. Black against gray, the colors of death. The unbearable colors of Mill- stown.

His throat tightened and his chest heaved. He tipped back his head and squeezed shut his burning eyes. Oh, God. He couldn't stand it. Not Norm, too...

He owed that man so much. Norm had plucked him off the fast track to prison. He'd taught him how decent people lived, what it meant to care. And now he was gone, gone like the rest of them...

A Canada goose honked overhead and Wade opened his eyes. He blinked to clear his vision as a vee of geese turned, then made a perfectly synchronized landing.

Despite the grief clenching his heart, Wade managed a smile. The damned geese made it look so easy. But for humans, a lot could go wrong during landing. He flexed his still-aching knee.

Even so, he loved that part of his job. Hurtling out the jump plane into the slipstream, floating silently above the earth under canopy. Jockeying the toggles, turning into the wind, the exhilaration of making the jump spot—at least sometimes.

A car door slammed and startled the geese. They waddled and flapped their wings, and lifted back into the sky. A fierce longing filled him, an overpowering urge to join them. He wanted desperately to get on his Harley and rip out of this wretched town.

But he couldn't leave Millstown yet. He owed Norm too much. And Erin. He couldn't ignore her plight.

"Wade Winslow." The acrid voice caught his attention and he slowly turned around. Battle-Ax Bester bore down on him, her thick, wide-shouldered body swathed in black. Her mouth curved down repressively and beneath her stiff hair, a permanent frown slashed her forehead.

She stopped several feet away. Her gaze flicked over him and her thin lips tightened down further. "Erin says you're staying at Mills Ferry."

He braced his hands on his hips. He wanted to ignore her. Her self-righteous proclamations had made his childhood hell. But this woman wielded power in Millstown. She could ruin Erin's standing in the community and create havoc with one nasty word.

"Just long enough to settle Norm's estate," he answered carefully.

"Well, see that you hurry. That girl doesn't need trouble, especially your kind." Her narrow gaze drove into his. "You look just like him, you know."

He knew who she meant. His father, the murderer. The man they all thought he'd become.

Anger surged and the muscles along his jaw tensed. They never gave up in this town, never forgot a bad reputation. "Believe me, I won't stay longer than I have to."

"Good." She turned and stalked away.

He struggled to hang on to his temper. He'd never had a chance in this town. Born into trash, destined to become a criminal. They had condemned him at birth. And until Norm intervened, he'd been hell-bent on proving them right.

But he agreed with her about one thing. Erin didn't need him in her life. The sooner he left, the better off she'd be.

A hand clamped his shoulder. Startled, he yanked his attention from Mrs. Bester's retreating back. A short, balding man with thick eyebrows stood at his side. Bob Hartman. The man who'd caught him breaking into his gas station years back and had him arrested. He braced himself for another blast.

"Sorry about Norm," Bob said instead.

The simple comment caught him off guard. "Thanks."

"Heard you're a smokejumper now."

"Yeah."

Bob squinted into the distance, his cheeks ruddy in

the brisk air, then looked at him again. "Norm told us about that. Sounds like you turned out good."

He blinked. Good? Strange word for anyone to connect to his name in this town.

"You staying here long?" Bob asked.

His shoulders tensed. "Just long enough to wrap things up."

"Too bad. If you decide to settle here, let me know. I'm thinking of selling the station. I figure it's time to put my feet up, let you young people run the town." He pumped his hand and walked off.

Wade snapped his jaw into place. Bob Hartman wanted to sell him his gas station. He thought Wade turned out well. Had someone's opinion of him actually changed in Millstown? Or had he misinterpreted what they'd originally thought?

That possibility jarred him. Mrs. Bester despised him; he hadn't imagined that. And there were plenty in Millstown like her. But maybe not everyone disliked him that much.

Still marveling over that concept, he glanced toward the road. A few people lingered by their cars, but most had left for Mills Ferry, where Erin had arranged a reception.

He didn't want to join them. The urge to flee surged back through him, a need to get on his V-Rod and ride. To crank back the throttle and let the speed and roar of the engine blast the grief from his mind.

But he couldn't do that right now. He had go to Mills Ferry and shake hands—for Erin's sake, and Norm's.

But not yet. He pulled his gaze to the edge of the

graveyard and sucked in an unsteady breath. He'd buried Norm today but hadn't put the whole past behind him. He still had something to face.

He tramped across the dry grass to the poorer, untended section of the cemetery bordering the woods. Simple, flat slabs marked the graves here instead of the sculpted headstones where Norm and Rose lay.

He stopped at a small stone barely visible through the weeds and flattened back the grass with his boot. His heart thudded in slow, thick beats as he read the faded inscription. *Leanne Winslow*. His mother.

No one had come to say goodbye to her that day, no one had cared, not even his father. Wade had huddled behind the bare trees, alone and afraid, while the workers had lowered her into the ground. After they'd left, he'd crept from the woods, flung himself over the grave and sobbed.

His chest cramped, and for one terrible moment, he was nine years old again, reliving the panic and fear. The helplessness, the resentment that had eventually grown into rage.

He frowned. He'd never realized that before, but it was true. He'd resented his mother's death. She'd left a scared, young boy with a dangerous man, and it had made him mad. Somehow, in his youthful mind, he'd believed that she'd done it on purpose.

And that anger had fueled his rebellion for years.

A movement caught his attention and he looked up. Erin stopped beside him. Her red hair blazed against her black wool coat and her freckles stood out in her face.

A sliver of warmth slid through his heart. She'd

stood at his side all morning, through the funeral at the church, the burial. But then, she'd always shown her unflagging support, even when others had shunned him.

She didn't speak right away. He liked that about her, that she sensed when he needed silence. Hell, why fool himself? He liked everything about her—being with her, looking at her, kissing her…

"I remember your mother," she finally said, her voice soft. "I saw her sometimes at the grocery store. She was pretty."

"Pretty tired was more like it since my old man didn't work." Just cashed in his unemployment checks and drank himself into a temper.

"At least she cared enough to support you."

"I guess." Although he hadn't seen her much. She'd cleaned motel rooms all day, then argued with his father all night—if the old man came home. Wade never knew why she cried if he didn't. At least then they got some sleep.

"My mother hardly thought about me after she dropped me off," Erin said. "I was lucky if she called at Christmas. And after a while, I couldn't even remember her much. When they told me she'd died in that accident, it was as if they were talking about a stranger." Her lips tightened. "I guess neither of us got lucky with parents."

"No." He hadn't chosen his parents, but the town still blamed him for them. But they'd never condemned Erin for hers. No one knew who her father was, although someone had paid to avoid a scandal. And once her mother had run through that cash, she'd unloaded Erin here.

So why hadn't they criticized Erin? Because her ancestors founded the town? He'd always figured that was the reason, but maybe his perception was off. After all, he'd apparently misjudged Bob Hartman.

Cold wind buffeted his face and Erin shivered beside him. Reaching over, he raised the collar on her worn, wool coat, then gently rubbed her shoulders. The woman needed warmer clothes, along with repairs to the house.

She needed money, period. And he seemed to be the only one willing to help her—which ticked him off considering all she did for this town.

Scowling, he dropped his hands. "Let's go over your books tonight."

"My what?"

"Your books. Your finances, to see how you're going to fund those repairs since you're so determined to stay in the house." And maybe he could find out exactly how broke she was.

"You don't have to worry," she said, her tone suddenly clipped. "I'm managing my money fine."

"That's not what I meant."

"Of course it is." Her pale cheeks flushed. "And believe me, I'm going to pay back that loan. Just because I can't do it yet—"

"For God's sake. Would you forget the damned loan?"

"No, I won't." She lifted her chin. "I owe you that money and I intend to pay it back."

The stubborn glint in her eyes sparked his temper. He'd never met anyone so independent. "Fine, if you're so bent on paying me back, then prove that you can do it. I'm sure you have some kind of plan?"

"Of course." She bit her lip.

He raised his brows.

"Fine," she snapped. "I'll show you the books."

"Good." He jammed his hands into his pockets. Why did she have to argue with everything? Why couldn't she cooperate for once?

Okay, so maybe she was right. He did want to check her expenses. But he was doing it for her own good. Why couldn't she let him help her?

Her long sigh cut through the silence and she lifted her gaze to his. "Listen, it's been a rough day. Let's not argue and make it worse."

Despite his annoyance, he knew she was right. He invariably made things worse. She stood by him, defended him, and all he did was hurt her.

But this time he'd get it right. He'd figure out a way to help her.

And then, like the geese, he would get out of Millstown and out of Erin's life.

Before he did something dangerous, like kiss her again.

"Where do you want this dish?"

Her hands in the sudsy water, Erin glanced back at Julie Brockman, her best friend and high school classmate. "Just set it on the table. I'll put it away later."

Lottie marched into the kitchen carrying two glasses. "This is it. Everything's done out there."

"Thanks, Lottie. Those should fit in the dishwasher." They'd finished the cleanup fast. Since the reception had been potluck, people had taken most of the dishes home.

"I'll help you with these pans," Julie said.

"Just leave them," Erin said. "They can dry where they are."

"But we're almost done." She picked up a dish towel and pulled a pan from the rack.

"Go on, let me handle that," Lottie said, snatching the towel from her hand. "You go on home to your kids. I don't have anything else to do since Mae's taking a nap."

Wishing she could nap, too, Erin fought back a wave of fatigue. Watching Wade suffer through the funeral had drained her. Oh, he'd masked his anguish well; he was a master at hiding emotions. But she knew how deeply he grieved. Even at his mother's grave she'd seen the pain in his eyes.

The buzz of a chain saw pulled her gaze to the window where Wade had strolled into view. Despite the cold weather, he wore a T-shirt with his faded jeans. The sweat-soaked shirt stretched tight as he cut a branch on the ground.

Awareness sparked through her nerves and her pulse tripped. Grieving or not, he was a gorgeous man, all muscles and masculine angles. She scanned the corded arms flecked with sawdust, the powerful back that tapered to his hard derriere, and felt her throat turn dry.

"...this week?"

She yanked her attention back to the kitchen. "What was that?"

"I asked if you're working at the Bonanza," Julie said.

"Oh. Yes, I'm selling raffle tickets during the Friday night basketball game."

"Good. I'll see you then." Julie picked up her bowl from the table, then slanted her a look. "You know, we haven't talked in a while. We need to go out for lunch."

Her casual tone didn't fool Erin. Julie, like everyone else in Millstown, thrived on gossip, and was dying to hear about Wade. "Maybe after I get my grades in. I'll have a breather then."

"Sure." Julie shrugged, undeterred. "I'll see you at the Bonanza."

"Give those kids a hug," Lottie told her.

"If they stand still long enough for me to catch them." Julie waved and left the kitchen.

Smiling, Erin poured the rinse water into a watering can to use on the drought-stricken bushes. She liked Julie, and they talked when they both had the time. But she didn't intend to discuss Wade with anyone. She'd never told Julie what happened in high school, never confided her feelings for Wade. And she didn't plan to start now.

Besides, the last thing Wade needed was more gossip. He'd suffered enough in this town.

Her gaze swiveled back to the yard, where he sawed another branch. His broad shoulders flexed and her heart made an unsteady jerk. He was an incredibly attractive man.

And that kiss had blasted her off her feet. She shivered, letting herself relive the fierce pleasure lashing her body, the heat of his big, rough hands on her skin. His rugged taste, his sensual smell.

That kiss had been better than she'd remembered, more exciting than she'd ever dreamed. She hadn't wanted to stop, couldn't have, if he hadn't pulled back.

And she'd give anything to kiss him again, which wouldn't be easy considering the rules he'd imposed on himself.

"...to bother you with this," Lottie was saying.

She dragged her attention to Lottie and blinked to clear her head. "I'm sorry, what did you say?"

Lottie dried a pot and set it on the counter. "I know this isn't a good time, what with Norm passing on and all. But I got a call from Terry this morning."

She frowned. Terry was Lottie's divorced daughter. She had two young girls to support, and a useless, dead-beat ex-husband.

"She just got laid off. They're closing the plant and taking the work to Mexico since labor's cheaper down there. I've been sending her money as it is, whatever I can spare every month, but now she's going to need more."

Erin rinsed the suds from the sink and dried her hands. Lottie didn't have much income, just her social security check, which was why their arrangement worked well. But if Lottie was sending the little she had to her daughter...

"She wants me to move down there to watch the girls while she looks for work, but I'd rather not. Not that I don't love those kids, but I'm too old to have them around all the time. And those Florida summers are hot. So I told her I'd send her money for day care. But I can only do that if I work at the hospital again."

The hospital? Erin froze.

"I hate to leave you in a lurch," Lottie continued. "I could still help Mae in the mornings if I work the late shift, but you'd have to find someone for the afternoons."

Panic clutched at her chest. She couldn't lose Lottie. The change would devastate Grandma.

She thought fast. Lottie needed money, so she had to pay her. But how? Did it matter? She had to keep Grandma with Lottie, no matter what the cost.

"I'll pay you whatever you need," she said. "I know the room isn't enough considering all you do."

"Nonsense. I don't work that many hours."

"No, no. I mean it. I've been intending to pay you all along. In fact, I mentioned that at the start."

"But I can't do that to you. You've got enough expenses." Lottie's faded blue eyes filled with tears.

Desperation surged. She had to convince Lottie to stay. "If you leave, I'll have to hire someone to take your place. And I'd much rather pay you. Besides, now that Wade's here, I've got plenty of money."

"I thought he was leaving soon."

"Oh, no. He's got months of work to do."

"But you need his money to fix the house."

"I've found another way to pay for that," she lied.

"Are you sure?"

"Absolutely." She pasted on a smile.

"All right then." Lottie hugged her, then dabbed the tears from her eyes.

"And we're all done here," Erin said. "Now you go put up your feet. You've done enough for today."

Lottie left and she turned back to the window. Oh, Lord. What was she going to do now? As long as Wade stayed, she could pay Lottie—instead of her other bills. But Lottie was right. Wade wouldn't stay here long. And what would she do when he left?

She knew one thing. She didn't dare tell him how

bad her finances were. Because he hadn't fooled her at all with that bit about fixing her house. He wanted to rescue her, solve all her problems, just as he had as a kid. And if he found out about Lottie, he'd feel even more obligated to help her.

She watched him saunter to a tree stump where he'd left a bottle of water. He set down the chain saw, then picked up the bottle and drank. Her gaze traced the dark stubble along his jaw to the solid lines of his neck, and everything inside her clenched.

It was so easy to fantasize about Wade, to dream of being wrapped in those arms. And not just for the sex, as thrilling as that would be. She was far more tempted to bury herself in his strength and let him take charge of her life.

But this was her house and her grandmother, and she had to solve her own problems.

Besides, despite that kiss, she knew Wade too well to build up any illusions. He couldn't stay in Millstown. She'd known that about him for years.

And yet… She studied the faded jeans hugging his muscled thighs, the damp shirt clinging to his back, and her breath wedged in her throat. That kiss had staggered her senses, awakened needs she'd buried for years.

And God help her, but she wanted to feel that again.

Wade wiped the sweat from his forehead with the sleeve of his T-shirt and eyed the scowling teen. Despite his mulish expression, Sean had hauled tree limbs for hours without complaining. Wade suspected the surly look was for show.

He should know. He'd spent years perfecting the same expression.

And it wasn't very appealing. He grimaced. No wonder no one had liked him much in this town.

"So what have you got after school tomorrow?" he asked.

Sean hunched his thin shoulders.

"No job? Sports?"

"No."

He nodded. "Fine. Be here right after school."

"What?" The kid's eyes flashed. "I already did your damned work."

"You did part of it," Wade corrected. "I'll tell you when you can stop."

Sean's scowl deepened and he jammed his hands into his pockets. As low and loose as the jeans hung, Wade was surprised they didn't fall off.

"I'll bring Norm's truck around so you can load up that wood," he added. He had to stop by the courthouse in the morning to file Norm's will, but later he could pick up the truck. He'd also get Norm's tree-climbing spurs so he could cut those dangling limbs.

Glad to be doing something constructive, he lifted the chain saw and fuel can, and headed to the storage shed. The hard, physical work had loosened his muscles and helped block the grief from his mind. He couldn't deal with the ache roiling through his chest just yet. The pain was too raw, too fresh. He'd rather concentrate on repairing the house and solving Erin's problems.

He stored the fuel and chain saw on a shelf and bolted the shed. Erin didn't want him fixing her problems. She didn't want him meddling in her life. And he didn't doubt she could manage her money.

But he knew her too well. She'd never ask for help. She'd never admit she needed anything unless he forced her.

And he was going to make her tell him the truth, whether she liked it or not.

Determined, he strode toward the house. Lottie rounded the corner as he approached the porch and hurried down the drive in his direction. He glanced at her tear-streaked face and the air stalled in his lungs. "What happened? Is it Erin?"

Lottie's watery gaze latched on his. "Oh, no, it's just… You're an angel. An absolute angel. I don't know what we'd do—" She covered her mouth with her hand and shook her head, then rushed past him toward the spring house.

He turned and frowned at her retreating back. An angel? Him? Who put that in her head?

He lifted his gaze to the house and saw Erin at the window. She immediately moved away, as if afraid he'd see her watching.

He stilled. Lottie had been talking to Erin. He'd bet his Harley on that. So why was she glad he was here?

A sick, sinking sensation soured his gut. He would discover the answer. He had no doubts about that. But he had a terrible suspicion he wasn't going to like it.

Chapter Seven

He didn't believe her. Her stomach clenched, Erin sat at her kitchen table late that night and watched Wade study her books. His dark brows gathered in concentration as he examined the doctored figures.

Her gaze lingered on his stubborn jaw, the implacable set to his shoulders, and she twisted her hands in her lap. She had to convince him that she had her finances under control. She absolutely could not let him know how deeply in debt she was sinking.

Because she knew him too well. Ever since they were kids, he'd tried to protect her. He'd chased off bullies and solved her problems. He'd even made sure her rare dates didn't cross any forbidden lines, or so she suspected.

Even that night at the river, he'd worked so hard to protect her. He'd been tender and patient, and so amazingly gentle that she'd cherished that memory for years.

And if he discovered the truth about her finances now, he'd feel obligated to stay and help her. He was just that kind of man. And she cared far too much for Wade to ever trap him in Millstown.

She tried to project an air of confidence. "As you can see, I can handle the routine expenses." Except for her bank loan, Lottie's salary, and her multiple credit card debts. "And as long as you're here, I'll use your rent to make repairs."

He leaned back in his chair. His whiskey-hued eyes skewered hers. "That's not going to pay for much."

"True, but I also plan to take out a bank loan." Another bank loan, she amended silently. "I tried getting money from the Historical Trust, but that's not going to work out."

"Why not?"

"Because to qualify for their loans, I'd have to give them a permanent easement."

His hard gaze stayed on hers. "Meaning?"

"That they'd take control of the house. They'd have to approve of any work around here. I'd have to submit photos and documentation before I could do anything, even paint."

"And that bothers you?"

"No, not exactly. They want to keep the house historically accurate, which is great. You know how I love history. But I can't afford to be authentic.

"Take the roof. They want me to use stamped tin, which is beautiful. I'd love to have it on the house. But a roof like that costs forty thousand dollars, maybe more. And that's just one repair. You saw the work this place needs."

Wade glanced back at the paper. "Well, I can't see the bank lending you much with your income."

She grimaced. "I know. I'd earn more if I could teach at the public school. I'd get better benefits, too. But those jobs are hard to come by. No one ever quits or retires."

"How about changing jobs?"

Her stomach plunged. "But I love teaching high school. It's what I've always wanted to do. Besides, I'm sure I can get the bank loan. I can use the house as collateral." And knowing Mike, the bank president's son, couldn't hurt.

Wade braced his arms on the table. "So, let me get this straight. You plan to take out a bank loan to pay me back and get money to fix the house."

"Right."

He gave her an incredulous look. "So how does that solve anything? You'll just have a bigger debt."

"Not that much bigger. Less than having a mortgage."

"But how will you make the payments? You're dead broke as it is."

Good question. "I can tutor more students."

"The hell you can. You're already exhausted."

"I'm fine. Things aren't as dire as you think." They were worse. Far worse. The sick churning in her stomach grew.

His sharp gaze pinned hers. Silence stretched between them and she nibbled her lower lip. She hated lying, especially to Wade. But she couldn't risk telling the truth.

"Lottie looked upset this afternoon," he said slowly.

Her pulse hitched. "I'm sure she was. Norm's death hit us hard."

"She seemed relieved that I was here."

Uneasiness seeped through her belly. "Lottie tends to overreact. I wouldn't pay any attention."

He leaned back, his gaze still riveting hers, and crossed his muscled arms. His black T-shirt stretched across his broad shoulders. For several seconds, he didn't speak.

"You remember when I threw that snowball at the school and broke the window?" he finally asked.

She blinked at the change of topic. "Sure, in the fifth grade."

"And you swore to Mr. Patton that I didn't do it."

"I said I didn't *see* you do it, which was technically true since I'd bent down to tie my shoe."

His eyes narrowed. "And then there was that time in, what was it, seventh grade? When you insisted I hadn't pulled the fire alarm?"

"You would have been suspended."

"I didn't care."

"Well, I did." She frowned. "So what's your point? That I lie a lot?"

"No, just the opposite. You're way too honest. So it's easy to tell when you're lying."

"Oh?"

"Yeah." He leaned forward. His gaze drilled into hers. "Every time you lie, you bite your bottom lip."

She snapped her mouth closed. The blasted man knew her too well. She rose and walked to the sink.

Wade's chair scraped back and suddenly he loomed beside her, his dark eyes far too astute. "So, you care to add anything to that list?"

"There's nothing else to add." She moved to the stove to check the timer.

"How about the truth?"

"I already gave it to you." Her stomach knotting, she grabbed the hot pads and opened the oven. She pulled out her chocolate-chip cookies and transferred them to the cooling rack, carefully avoiding his eyes.

Praying he'd let the subject drop, she refilled the cookie sheet, then braved a glance in his direction. He leaned against the counter, his arms crossed. Frustration brewed in his eyes.

"Look," he said. I'm not the enemy here. I'm only trying to help you."

"I know." And she was protecting him.

"You might as well tell me the truth. I'm not going to let this go."

She knew that, too. But he couldn't force her to talk. "Don't eat too many of these cookies," she warned. "They're for the Fire and Rescue bake sale."

"Hell." Scowling ominously now, he braced his hands on his hips. "That's another thing that bugs me. You work too hard around here. From what I heard at that reception today, you volunteer for everything."

"So?" She slid the cookie sheet into the oven and reset the timer.

"So you're exhausted. You're thin and pale, and you've got circles under your eyes."

"I'll survive." She set the hot pads on the counter. "Besides, I like doing my part in the community."

"Yours and everyone else's."

"I don't do that much."

"No? Let's see what you're doing this month." He

held up his hand to count. "First there's the high school Bonanza and this bake sale for the Rescue Squad. Then there's the Thanksgiving food drive, the Christmas toy drive, some fund-raiser for the battered women's shelter—"

"Okay, fine. So I do too much. But I can't let everyone down."

"Why not? I didn't hear anyone at that reception offering to help you back."

"Because they need me. And I'd feel terrible saying no." An edgy, panicked feeling crept through her gut, but she firmly pushed it aside. She didn't need to turn anyone down. She could handle these projects fine.

"And I don't care if they help me or not," she added. "I'm not keeping score."

"Well, maybe you should start." His heated gaze held hers. "When do you have time for fun?"

"Fun?"

"Yeah, fun. You know, after you've worked and volunteered, and taken care of your grandmother?"

She shrugged.

"You do remember what fun is?"

Oh, yes. Her gaze dropped to his mouth. Kissing Wade had been fun. And thrilling.

And she would love to do it again. She licked her lips, then swallowed hard.

She dragged her gaze back to his. His brown eyes narrowed and darkened. Tension rolled off his body. And he stood perfectly still.

Her pulse leaped with an answering hunger. She wanted to kiss him again. To feel that excitement, that heat rushing through her. That wild desire sizzling her blood.

Somehow, he'd moved closer. Much closer. Her heart hammered when his breath fanned her face. "Was kissing me fun?" he asked, his voice low.

A thrill ran through her. She tried to speak, but failed.

He reached out and cupped her neck, sliding his rough, warm hand down her skin. She shivered at the sparks coursing through her.

His eyes were hard now, dangerous, and she couldn't look away. He grasped her arms and urged her closer. Her heart rioted in her chest.

"Tell me, Erin," he rasped again. "Just how much fun was it?"

She parted her lips, but nothing came out. She dropped her gaze to his mouth, then lifted it helplessly back to his eyes. She felt his intensity, his heat. Her knees grew suddenly weak.

And then he lowered his head and his lips covered hers, hard and warm and seeking. With a moan, she wrapped her arms around his strong neck and surrendered to her desire.

Oh, how she ached for this man. She'd longed for him, yearned for him. She'd wanted to touch him and stroke him forever.

She caressed the rough, sexy stubble of his jaw and threaded her hand through his hair. She explored the hard width of his shoulders, marveling at his raw strength.

His tongue stroked her lips, demanding acceptance. She opened gladly, welcoming the sensual invasion. He made a low, deep sound in his throat and sharp pleasure shocked her to her toes.

And she tried to get even closer. She tightened her hold on his neck. His hands roamed her back, her buttocks, sending shivers of pleasure shooting through her. He lifted her slightly and pressed her against his arousal. Heat coiled between her legs, desire so fierce that she moaned.

She wanted him to touch her. Desperately. All over her naked body. To yank off their clothes and absorb him into her skin.

To relive, for one blissful moment, that ecstasy she'd known years ago.

But without warning, he lifted his head. Bereft, she opened her eyes. Her heart thundered. Her head spun. Their breathing rasped loud in the silence.

His gaze burned into hers, almost angry in its intensity. "This doesn't solve a damn thing," he said. He pulled her arms from his neck and stepped back.

Suddenly dizzy, she clutched the counter for balance. Her mind blank, her body throbbing, she watched him cross the kitchen.

At the doorway, he stopped, turned and nailed her with his gaze. "And when we make love," he said, his voice raw, "it's going to be a hell of a lot more than just fun."

Chapter Eight

"Here you go, Mr. Herter." Raising her voice to be heard above the roar in the high school gymnasium, Erin tore three raffle tickets from the roll and handed them to the elderly gentleman perched on the wooden bleachers. "Good luck." She stuck his dollar bill into the pocket of the apron she wore over her jeans, then searched the crowd for Wade.

Her hopes sank when she didn't see him. He probably wouldn't come. And why should he? He didn't have fond memories of high school. And he certainly didn't want to spend time with her lately. They'd hardly spoken since that last kiss.

"Hi, Erin." She turned at the tap on her shoulder.

Her friend, Julie, handed her a dollar. "You'd better sell me the winner," Julie teased. "Joey's counting on this ball."

"I'll try." Joey, Julie's oldest, loved sports. "So where are the kids, anyway?"

"Getting hot dogs." Julie stuffed the tickets in her purse and leaned forward. Her straight, blond hair swung over her shoulders. "Listen, what's this I hear about Wade still staying at your house?"

Erin kept her expression blank. Julie meant well, but the woman loved to gossip. And she wasn't about to provide her with news. "That's right. He's renting a room until he cleans out Norm's duplex."

Julie raised her brows. "Jeez, do you think that's safe? I mean, he was always so wild. And his father murdered a man."

Erin felt her face heat. "His father, not him. And it was manslaughter, a fight in a bar, not premeditated murder."

"I know, but still, you have to wonder. I mean, I know he's gorgeous and all, but what if there's some sort of genetic or environmental—"

"Julie!" Erin frowned at her friend. "Wade wouldn't hurt anyone. How can you even suggest that?"

"But you haven't seen him in years. How do you know what he'd do?"

"Because I know Wade. He hasn't changed that much. And believe me, I'm perfectly safe." Except from his kisses, but Julie didn't need to know that.

"If you say so." Julie's blond brows furrowed. "I just don't want to see you hurt."

"I won't be." Fortunately, the high school principal strolled by just then, giving her an excuse to bolt. "Excuse me, Julie, but I need to talk to Mr. Reginski. I'll see you later."

She hurried to catch up with the principal, her stomach still churning with indignation. People had always misunderstood Wade. No one saw his good side, his honest and generous nature.

Because Wade had never let them see that side. He'd only shown them what they'd expected, so naturally, they'd thought the worst.

She caught up with the principal and stopped. "Hello, Mr. Reginski. Raffle tickets for the game ball?" She held up the roll of tickets, sure he'd spring for one in front of the crowd.

"You know," she added as he dug into his pocket and handed her a crumpled bill, "I'd still like to teach here if a position opens up."

"I thought you were working at St. Michaels."

"Just as a long-term sub." She ripped three tickets off the roll and handed them over. "I'd much rather work here if I could. You know how I love this school."

He slipped the tickets into his shirt pocket and frowned. "And I'd like to hire you, but I don't think anyone's leaving."

"Well, I'd appreciate it if you'd keep me in mind if they do."

"Of course."

She sighed as he walked away. That was the problem in Millstown. With jobs this scarce, especially good ones with benefits, people clung to theirs for life. She'd been lucky to find the temporary job at St. Michaels.

The half-time horn blasted and the crowd clapped as the players jogged off the court toward the locker rooms. The announcer's voice echoed through the gym.

Erin glanced at her watch and stifled a yawn. Mike would be taking over the raffle now, thank goodness. She was beat. Unless Wade came, she'd go straight home to bed. She scanned the crowded bleachers again.

The cheerleaders pranced onto the court in their blue and white uniforms and gave a brief, unsynchronized cheer. She sold a few more tickets while she watched for Mike, finally spotting him near the stage. Relieved, she walked over and untied her apron.

He smiled as she approached. "How's business?" He took the apron and tied it around his own lean waist. He wasn't as tall or muscular as Wade, but had friendly blue eyes and hair that receded only slightly.

"Pretty good. You might start on that side." She motioned to the opposite bleachers. Still hopeful, she searched the crowd for Wade again, then eyed the entrance where a group of girls lingered.

"…next week?"

"Sorry?" She turned back to Mike. He took her arm and pulled her to the corner of the bleachers, where the crowd noise was partially blocked.

"I asked if you wanted to have dinner next week," he said.

"Dinner?" A sick feeling unfurled in her stomach. Mike was asking her for a date. She couldn't ignore the truth or chalk his interest up to friendship any longer.

And she had to face facts. She didn't want a romantic relationship with Mike. Not after Wade's kiss. Not after she'd felt that excitement. She couldn't fool herself ever again.

Or Mike. He deserved the truth. She inhaled deeply, dreading the confrontation. "Mike, I'm sorry." She searched for the kindest words. "You're a great friend and I don't want to hurt you, because I really like you a lot. But I... I just think of you as a friend."

Hurt flashed through his eyes and she winced. She knew it sounded lame, but it was true. He was a wonderful man, and he'd make some woman a great husband—just not her.

"It's Winslow, isn't it?" he asked.

"No."

"He won't hang around for long."

"I know that. I never expected him to. And it isn't because of Wade."

Mike shoved his hand through his hair. "For God's sake, Erin. The man jumps out of planes for a living and rides around on a Harley. You don't need a guy like that."

"It's really not because of Wade," she insisted. And Mike was wrong. She did need Wade, desperately. But she also knew she couldn't have him.

But those kisses had shattered her complacency. She'd felt passion—searing, staggering passion—for the first time in twelve long years. And now she couldn't settle for less.

Whether or not Wade stayed.

"Well, don't say I didn't warn you," he muttered.

She eased out her breath. "I'm hereby forewarned."

"And if you ever need a shoulder to cry on..." He slung his arm around her shoulder and squeezed.

"Thanks, but I won't."

At least she hoped not.

Wade shifted down a gear, slowed his Harley to a pulsing rumble, and turned into the high school parking lot. His headlight flashed over rows of cars and pickups.

Unease gripped his gut. He shouldn't have come. He had no business being near Erin. Hadn't he just spent the past week making sure he kept his distance?

But he couldn't fool himself anymore. That kiss had razed his illusions. Even after all these years, he wanted her. The need grew worse every day. And he couldn't trust himself to keep his damned hands off her.

He punched the Harley's throttle, surged to the end of the lot, then braked by the statue of James Buchanan and cut the engine. But unwise or not, he had to see her tonight. And the high school gym would be a safe, public place.

He got off his bike and set the kickstand, then pulled off his helmet and slung it over the backrest. The smell of cigarettes pulled his attention to a group of boys slouched against the statue.

They gazed back at him, their expressions carefully sullen. He'd been like that as a kid, skulking in the dark and acting tough. But had he really looked that young?

"Hey, you're that smokejumper guy, aren't you?" one kid asked.

"Yeah." He unzipped his jacket and pulled off his gloves.

"Cool. Nice bike," the kid added. The other boys straightened and edged closer.

He understood their dilemma. They wanted desperately to see the bike, but showing their interest wasn't cool.

"Hey, Wade." Sean stepped from behind the statue

and swaggered over, acting nonchalant in front of his friends.

"Sean," he acknowledged. "You coming by the house tomorrow?"

Awe slackened the ring of faces. By knowing Wade, Sean had gained instant prestige.

He shook his head. That had to be a first in this town.

"Probably. Yeah." Sean struggled not to beam.

"Good. See you then." He strolled up the sidewalk to the gym, leaving Sean to explain their relationship however he wanted. When he reached the door, he glanced back. The boys were clustered around the Harley, gesturing with excitement.

Walking into the lobby thrust him back twelve years. The familiar smell of hot dogs drifted from the concession stand. Tennis shoes squeaked in the gym, along with the thundering of running players. The referee's whistle pierced the spectators' roar.

He scanned the lobby, looking for Erin. Standing by the gym door, a group of girls in tight jeans tossed their hair over their shoulders and sent him inviting glances.

He blinked. Had he really lusted after girls that young in high school? He was starting to feel ancient.

"Hey, Winslow! Is that you?" He turned. Butch Ableson, his former classmate and cohort in crime, grinned up at him. They'd been regulars at Saturday detention for years, pushing brooms down halls and scraping gum off the desks. He grinned back and shook his hand.

"Heard you were in town," Butch said. "You're staying at Erin's, right?"

"Yeah. She's renting me a room." He knew he had to make that clear.

"You staying long?"

"Just long enough to sell Norm's house and tie up loose ends." Which could be quite a while, he'd discovered at the courthouse this week. Dying created an incredible amount of paperwork.

Butch frowned. "That's too bad. We could use you at the fire department. Chief Hancock's retiring this year."

"Thanks, but I'm not staying."

"Well, if you change your mind, let me know. You got time to hunt while you're here?"

"Maybe. If Norm's still got his guns."

"Give me a call if you're interested." Butch clapped his shoulder and turned away.

Still smiling, Wade wound through the crowded lobby to the gym. He fished a few bucks from his pocket, paid the woman sitting at the table by the door, then got the back of his hand stamped.

The woman beside her gaped at him. She looked familiar, but he couldn't place her. With a mental shrug, he turned away.

"Do you know who that is?" He heard her say to the other woman. "Wade Winslow! His father killed a man…"

And without warning, the past came crashing back and he heard the accusing voices.

"…murderer's son."

"…not decent."

"Winslows…white trash. Run the whole bunch out of town."

"I'll whip you if you go near him again."

"Killer!"

Shame burned through his blood and for a terrible moment he was a kid again. The outcast. The town pariah. Drawing stares and whispers wherever he went. And constant condemnation.

He dragged a hand over his face. *Hell.* No wonder he hated this town. No one ever forgot the past. Even after all these years, they still blamed him, even for things that weren't his fault.

No, that wasn't true, he now had to admit. Some people did accept him. Butch Ableson, Bob Hartman from the gas station. Erin…

He thought of those boys at the statue. Maybe his perception really had been skewed back then. Maybe he'd just assumed that nobody liked him. He had been awfully young. And maybe he'd been partly to blame, since he hadn't tried to fit in.

More thoughtful now, he entered the gym and walked along the endline, staying close to the wall to avoid the players scrabbling for the ball. He inhaled the smell of floor wax and sweat, and scanned the crowded bleachers for Erin. He finally spotted her by the stage across the gym. Her red hair glowed against her black sweater and his pulse kicked up a notch.

She stood beside a blond man of medium height. He frowned. Mike Kell. The man who wanted to date her.

They turned slightly. Mike had his arm looped over her shoulder. Wade felt his face grow hot. A dull roar buzzed in his head.

Then Mike bent and kissed her.

Anger pooled in his belly, then burst in a hot, rushing blaze. Twelve years ago he'd left Millstown, thinking she needed a better man. But he'd never actually pictured her with anyone else. He'd always blocked that image out.

The reality stunned him. Shocked him. Filled him with possessive rage.

And forced him to face another cold truth. He couldn't let another man have her. He wanted her for himself.

But he didn't have that right. Erin wasn't his, and never would be.

Suddenly she looked at him and their gazes locked.

He clenched his hands into fists. He couldn't take this. He couldn't stand here and watch her with another man. His vision hazing, he turned and strode out the door.

A crowd blocked the exit from the lobby, so he headed down the hallway leading into the school. He walked blindly past clusters of lockers, not caring where he went. He just needed to get away.

"Wade!" Erin called from behind him. He walked faster, his boots sharp on the tile floor.

"Wade, wait!" She caught up with him and tugged his arm.

He stopped. She was panting, her face pink from running across the gym. She looked so beautiful that his chest hurt.

"Where are you going? I was waiting for you," she said.

"Yeah?" He kept his expression blank.

"Listen, that kiss wasn't what you think. Mike was just being friendly."

"None of my business what you do."

"But I told you before, we're not dating."

"Fine. You're not dating." He pulled his arm free and strode off.

She ran around him and blocked his way. "Could you wait?" she asked. "I'd like to talk."

Talk? Hell, he wanted to slam his fist through the wall. "Not now."

"But you've been avoiding me all week."

Damn right he had. He hadn't trusted himself around her. And he had to get away from her now.

He tried to step around her, but she moved into his path. "Wade, please."

His anger building, he braced his hand on the wall and sucked in air. His face felt hot. His blood coursed hard in his ears. And he was fast spiraling out of control.

"Wade?" She rested her hand on his arm.

"For God's sake, Erin," he pleaded, his voice raw. "Can't you leave me alone?"

"No, I can't. I need to exp—"

He pushed away from the wall. "Damn it, Erin! Just what the hell do you want from me?" Did she think he was superhuman?

Her gaze dropped to his mouth and his self-control slipped even further. "Another kiss, is that it? What am I, some sort of toy?"

"No," she gasped, turning pale. "I'd never do that to you."

"So what do you want then? Sex? Is that it?"

She shook her head. "No, I—"

"Fun. You want some fun, right? More fun than

you'd have with Mike?" Furious now, he backed her against the wall. And watched her lick her lips.

And suddenly he lost it. He grabbed her waist and yanked her to him, then ground his lips against hers. He devoured her mouth, plundering wildly, invading her warm, wet depths with his tongue.

His control cracked; his careful defenses shattered. He vented his anger, his passion, his need.

And staked absolute possession. She was his. Only his. And he'd be damned if he'd let Mike have her.

He reached up to grasp her head, then fisted his hands in her hair. He was too rough, too wild, and he knew it, but hunger knotted his guts. The blood slammed through his veins with desire so raw that it shocked him.

Erin. He needed Erin. Right now. Right here. And he couldn't make himself stop.

His world blurred. He felt dazed, immobile, as though he were free-falling ninety miles an hour toward certain death and couldn't deploy his reserve. And he didn't care. He only kissed her deeper and harder.

And groaned when she kissed him back.

He inhaled her sultry perfume and the soft, sweet scent of her skin. Slid his hands down her back and cupped the full, lush curves of her bottom. Felt the fierce ache jolt through his groin and pulled her tightly against him.

And he couldn't stop. His pulse thundered. His focus narrowed to his violent need. He knew he was reckless and rough, and far too close to the edge, but he couldn't stop kissing Erin.

And that annoyed him even more.

Making one last stab at control, he jerked up his head. "If you want sex," he rasped, "you've got it. But that's all this is, just sex."

He clenched her hair. He felt furious with her. And at himself for wanting her so much. "Do you understand that?"

Her lips were swollen, her cheeks raw where his whiskers had scratched her. Tears welled in her luminous eyes.

His anger abruptly deflated, replaced with remorse. "Oh, hell. I hurt you." Hurt her? He'd acted like a bloody animal. With Erin! Fierce guilt swamped his gut.

He braced his hands on the wall behind her and hung his head, ashamed. What had he been thinking? How could he have lost control?

"Oh, God, Erin," he murmured. "I'm sorry."

"I'm okay," she said, her voice husky.

He shook his head. He couldn't justify his behavior. There was no excuse for the way he'd acted.

"You didn't hurt me," she said again. "It was just so wonderful that I…"

"Aw, Erin." How typical of her, to make excuses for his bad behavior. He brushed the tears from her cheeks with his thumbs and took her gently into his arms. He cradled her head against his chest and berated his loss of control.

And the worst part was that he was still violently aroused, still wanted desperately to drive into her and slake his need. Hell, he wanted her so much he was shaking.

He tipped his head back in self-disgust. What kind of barbarian was he? Why couldn't he control this lust?

And why couldn't he have sex with this woman? Just give in to this need and forget it? He could be casual with anyone else.

But with Erin, everything was complicated, confusing. But what made her so different?

Suddenly he heard footsteps behind him. His heart tanked. He turned slightly to shelter Erin, but knew that it was too late.

And there was no doubt about what they'd been doing. Erin looked ravaged. Her lips were red and swollen, her sweater askew. Her hair floated wildly around her face.

The steps abruptly halted and someone gasped. Dread chugged through his gut and he slowly turned his head. And then he groaned.

Mrs. Bester and Mr. Paddack—the town's worst gossip and Erin's boss from St. Michaels—stood rooted, their mouths agape.

He closed his eyes, knowing he deserved to be shot. Not only had he hurt Erin tonight, but he'd just demolished her reputation in the community.

Chapter Nine

Erin paused outside the principal's office and pulled in a breath. She'd dreaded this summons all weekend, ever since Mr. Paddack had seen her kissing Wade at the Bonanza on Friday night. Frankly, she was surprised he'd waited until the end of the school day to call her in.

And she knew exactly what was coming, a lecture on public decorum. Which was ironic, since she was normally private about personal matters. But she hadn't acted reserved Friday night. And in the process, she'd set a poor example for the students and made St. Michaels look bad.

But she certainly didn't regret that kiss. She closed her eyes, reliving the wildness, the urgency in Wade's lips. The power in his hard, warm hands. The thrills shooting over her body.

And when he'd lost control… She shivered. She hadn't felt that excited in years. Twelve long years, to be exact.

With a sigh, she opened her eyes. That kiss had kept her awake for the past three nights, wriggling and turning in bed. Even the sound of Wade's footsteps in the hall made her pulse sprint.

But as electrifying as that kiss had been, she'd done it in a public place. And that was wrong. All she could do now was apologize, weather Mr. Paddack's lecture, and then get back to work. She rapped on the office door.

"Come in."

Mr. Paddack sat at his desk, riffling through papers. "Good afternoon. You wanted to see me?" She hesitated near the door.

The principal removed his reading glasses and looked up. "Have a seat, Erin." He motioned her to a padded chair in front of his desk. While she sat, he folded his glasses and set them deliberately on the stack of papers.

She waited for him to speak. His sober expression made her chest clench. The teachers called him "Paddy-whack" because he twiddled his thumbs when he was upset. The thumbs rolled steadily now.

After a long moment he shifted, making his leather chair creak. "You know, I've been very pleased with your performance here. You came in at a difficult time, and you've done an admirable job for our history department."

"Thank you," she murmured, waiting for the "but" she heard in his voice.

"But," he continued on cue, "I have to admit I was shocked by your behavior Friday night."

She cringed. "Yes, I know."

"You realize that this is a conservative parochial school," he said. His thumbs twirled faster.

"Of course."

"And you signed an agreement promising to uphold our values. It was one of the conditions of your employment."

"I know that." She lifted a hand. "But I hardly think one kiss qualifies as immoral behavior."

"One very public kiss. And I also understand that you're living together."

Her breath stalled. "Oh, no. That's not true."

"That man's not staying at your house?"

"Well, yes. Wade's renting a room, but it's not like we… Well, you know. We're not…"

Mr. Paddack lifted his brows.

Her face flamed. How could she deny that she and Wade were intimate? Anyone who'd seen that kiss would reach that obvious conclusion.

The principal leaned back in his chair. "You need to understand my position. I'm not trying to dictate your behavior, but this is a private school. Parents send their children here to foster a moral lifestyle. Teachers can't act in a way that goes against the purpose of the school."

His chair creaked again. "And we've already received a complaint about your behavior. The president of the school board phoned me today."

Someone had complained? She stiffened. "Who? Mrs. Bester?" That woman was the worst kind of gossip. "But she's always—"

"It doesn't matter who called. Rumors like this are bad for us, no matter where they come from. We don't receive government funds here. We depend on the students' tuition. And if parents pull out their children…"

A sick dread trickled through her belly. Exactly what was he saying?

"So if you want to keep your position, there can be no more displays like the one you put on Friday night. And move that man out of your house."

Her heart jerked. "Move him out? But he's renting a room. I can't tell him to leave."

"I'm sorry, but you don't have a choice. We can't afford the scandal."

She gaped at him. He was serious. He really wanted her to make Wade leave.

A horrible, sinking feeling filled her chest. She could never tell Wade to move out. Never. Not after the rejection he'd faced as a child. He'd spent his entire life believing that he was an outcast, that no one wanted him here.

That no one cared.

And that the few people who did care—his mother, Rose, and Norm—abandoned him anyway, through death.

She was his only friend left. And she would never betray that friendship. Never. Not even for the sake of her job.

Not even to keep her grandmother's house?

Panic roiled through her belly. How could she pay Lottie if she lost her job? Or the mounting medical bills?

Unless she sold Mills Ferry… But it would kill her grandmother to move!

But she could never forsake Wade. The nausea in her stomach swelled. "I can't do that," she whispered.

Mr. Paddack tilted his head. "I'm very sorry to hear that, but it's your decision, of course. Naturally, since your work has been excellent, I'll write you a letter of recommendation. This shouldn't affect your employment in the public schools."

A letter of recommendation. The blood drained from her face. "Exactly what are you saying?"

"That at the end of this semester, your contract won't be renewed."

"Do you really jump into fires?"

Wade set his water bottle on the ground beside his chain saw and grinned at the kid who'd asked the question. "Only if I've completely screwed up. The spotter puts us down near the fire, not in it."

The boys clustered closer around him. Ever since the basketball game Friday night, the ragtag group of teens had shown up at Mills Ferry every afternoon to help Sean clean up the yard. Today they'd finally gathered their courage and started pestering him with questions.

"That must be cool to jump out of a plane," the kid, Jay, said.

Wade studied the kid. He was tall, with the lanky lines of a still-growing teenager. But his wide shoulders would eventually broaden to a powerful build. And despite his pierced eyebrow and spiked hair, there was an intensity about him that reminded Wade of himself.

"I was scared as hell the first time I did it," he admitted. "But I was even more afraid that I'd let down my bros. Those are the guys you jump with. There was no way I was going to freeze in the door and disappoint them like that."

And that was what kept him jumping. His bros, the people he could depend on. The camaraderie and sense of belonging he'd never had growing up.

"Doesn't it hurt when you land?" Sean asked.

"Not if you do it right. But anything can happen." And every year, it took longer to recover from the injuries. He flexed his still-aching knee. "You're more likely to hang up in a tree."

"What do you do if that happens?"

"Take out your let-down rope and get down as fast as you can. You don't want to be stuck in a tree with a forest fire burning nearby."

A car passed on the road that fronted Mills Ferry, catching his attention. He glanced at his watch and frowned. Where was Erin? She should have come back hours ago. In fact, she'd been arriving home late all week.

He propped his hands on his hips, thinking hard. Something was wrong; he could feel it. Something that had distracted her, making her nervous and distant for days.

The kiss? Was she avoiding him because of that? His jaw hardened. When she came home, he was going to ask.

He tugged his keys from his pocket. "Anybody want to drive the truck over so we can load up this wood?"

"I'll do it," Sean said.

"Can you drive a stick?"

"Sure."

He doubted the kid even had a license, but he couldn't do much damage driving Norm's old truck across the lawn. "Back it up to the trees," he said, and tossed him the keys. Grinning, Sean trotted off toward the driveway.

"So, is it hard to become a smokejumper?" Jay persisted.

Wade picked up his chain saw and moved it aside. "Yeah, it's tough. A lot of guys wash out of rookie training."

"But you made it."

"Yeah." It wasn't hard to imagine what Jay was thinking. If another poor kid from Millstown had made it, maybe he could, too. "But you have to have some firefighting experience before you apply," he cautioned. "Forest fires, like on a hotshot crew. That's what I did after high school."

"What's that?" another kid named Alex asked.

"The hotshots get trucked in after the jumpers to help fight the bigger fires. But you have to be eighteen to be a hotshot."

"I'll be eighteen in March," Jay said.

He watched Sean lurch the truck across the lawn, then back awkwardly up to the trees. He turned to the group of teens. "I'll tell you what. I need help fixing this place up. Any of you want a job, I'll hire you. You show me you can work hard, that you're dependable, and I'll see about getting you on a hotshot crew this summer."

"Me, too?" another kid asked.

"Anyone who's old enough and willing to do the work."

"Cool!"

The truck jolted to a stop and Sean hopped out, rubbing his jaw to hide his wide grin. Wade strode over and let down the tailgate. By the time he'd turned around, the boys had already started hauling logs to the truck, rushing to show how hard they could work.

They were unloading the last few logs beside the toolshed when Erin finally drove up. Wade watched her step out of the battered Honda, then reach back for a bag of groceries, her movements stiff. She glanced in his direction, then looked away.

His gaze hardened. Something was wrong, all right. And whatever it was, he was going to find out. She wasn't going to avoid him this time.

He slammed the tailgate shut and removed his leather work gloves. "Anybody who's got clean boots can carry groceries into the house. Then we're done for the day."

"Sure, Wade."

The boys hurried over to the car. Erin handed one boy her bag, then walked around and opened the trunk. Wade strode over and joined them.

"Leave these three bags here." She pointed to the sacks in the back of the trunk. "They're for the canned food drive. You can put the rest on the kitchen counter. Just go in the back door. There's an entrance to the kitchen off the porch."

She dug through a few bags, then looked up. "This one's heavy. It's the turkey."

"I'll carry it," Sean said.

"Like hell you will." Jay nudged him aside.

Wade frowned. "Hey, watch your language around a lady."

A flush crept up Jay's neck. "Sorry," he mumbled to Erin.

"That's okay." She moved aside while the boys unloaded the groceries, then leaned against the car and crossed her arms. "You don't," she said when the kids were out of earshot.

He stepped close. The circles under her eyes looked darker. "I don't what?"

"Watch your language."

"Sure I do."

She shook her head, making her red hair shimmer in the fading afternoon light. Even tired, she was beautiful. More than he'd remembered through the years. And he'd pictured her often enough. Every time he'd crawled under his tarp after fighting fire, hovering on the verge of exhaustion. That time his main chute had malfunctioned and he'd had to employ his reserve. And every damned time he'd been with another woman, he'd thought about Erin. Always Erin.

Unable to resist, he reached out and stroked the soft curve of her cheek, then cupped his hand on her neck. Her pulse sped beneath his palm. His gaze dropped to her lips and the breath stuck in his throat.

"You mean, you swear even worse when I'm not around?" she asked, her voice hoarse.

"Hell, yes."

Her lips curved into a smile, but immediately sagged again. Anxiety flitted through her tired eyes.

He tilted up her chin. "What's wrong?"

"Nothing." She scooted away, then started up the back path toward the house.

His frustration surging, he followed. "Come on, Erin. I'm not blind. Something's bothering you."

"I'm fine. Really."

"Then why are you avoiding me? Was it that kiss?"

"No!" She stopped with her hand on the porch door and turned back. Her eyes met his. "I'd never regret that. That was—" her voice dropped "—amazing."

His pulse jerked, then hammered in his chest, and his gaze fell to her lips. Amazing was right. That kiss had aroused him out of his mind.

The clomp of heavy footsteps interrupted that thought. Erin held open the door and the teens piled out.

"Thanks, guys," she said.

"You're welcome, Ms. McCuen."

"'Bye, Wade. See you tomorrow."

He waited as the kids trooped by, impatient at the interruption. But when the last kid tramped past, Erin slipped inside the porch and disappeared.

Annoyed, he swung open the door and followed. So if the kiss wasn't bothering her, what was? She could try to dodge his questions, but he still planned to find out the truth.

But when he strode into the kitchen, Lottie and Mrs. McCuen were sitting at the table. Erin bent and gave her grandmother a hug.

"Just leave the groceries for now," she said to Lottie. "I'll put everything away in a minute. I'm going to give Grandma a bath if you can hold off on dinner for a while."

Her gaze lifted to his. "Do you mind waiting a few minutes to eat?"

"Of course not." He scowled. But if she thought he was letting her slave over dinner after working all day, she was nuts. The woman was exhausted enough.

"Thanks, Erin," Grandma murmured as Erin helped her to her feet. "Did you go to the bank like I asked you?"

"Yes, Grandma. Everything's fine." Erin carefully braced her grandmother against her, then slowly walked with her to the hall.

Wade slammed his fist against his palm, his frustration building. She could try to avoid him, but it wasn't going to work.

He stalked to the refrigerator, yanked it open and pulled out a can of the beer he'd stocked. Then he turned to face Lottie. "What do you like on your pizza?"

"Pizza?" The woman's mouth sagged. "Why, everything, but I don't think Erin—"

"Erin has nothing to do with it. I'm buying." He pulled the tab on his beer and took a long swig. "There still that Pizza Shack up by the highway?"

"Yes."

He walked over to the phone book on the end of the counter and flipped through the pages. "Anything Erin's grandma can't eat?"

"Well, peppers don't set too well with her anymore."

He pulled the phone off the hook, punched in the number and told them to deliver two large pizzas, one with everything on it, and the other without the peppers. Then, with dinner taken care of, he took another slug of beer and turned back to Lottie. Maybe Erin wouldn't tell him what was bothering her, but he still intended to get some answers.

He narrowed his gaze on the woman. "I'm worried about Erin," he said bluntly.

"Erin?" Her eyes widened. "Whatever for?"

"You tell me. She looks worried lately. Is there something wrong with her grandmother?"

"Oh, no." She shook her head, making her gray curls bounce. "Mae's improving every day. Well, she's still convinced the bank's stealing her money, of course. And her memory's bad, but she was forgetful before the accident. That's probably what caused it. She shouldn't have been driving anymore, but she was always stubborn and independent."

Traits Erin had definitely inherited. He took another long swallow of beer and drained the can. He strode over to the trash and tossed it in. "Would you like a beer?"

Lottie's face lit up. "Why, yes. Thank you."

Wade retrieved two more cans from the refrigerator. "You want a glass?"

"Yes, please."

Wade set down the cans, got the glass, then eased himself into a chair across from Lottie. "I guess it must be the money that's got her worried, then."

"Oh, no. I'm sure that's not it."

He watched her pour her beer into the glass. "The house needs a lot of work."

"But she's found a way to pay for that." She smiled. "She told me so herself. That's why she could pay me."

Wade leaned back in his chair and folded his arms. "What do you mean?"

Lottie sipped her beer, then dabbed at her lips with a napkin. "At the beginning, I took care of Mae in exchange for room and board, which was more than generous. I don't do that much around here. And I could get by fine on my social security check. But last week my daughter got laid off… Well, you don't want to hear about that. But I was going to have to get another job to earn more money."

He narrowed his eyes. The connection between her daughter and job had lost him, but one thing was definitely clear. "So Erin's paying you a salary now." And Lottie had called him an angel. *Oh, hell.* "And she's using my rent to pay you."

"Yes, that's right. She said she didn't need it for anything else."

Like hell she didn't. The woman was flat-out broke.

His stomach churned at the implications. Erin needed his rent to pay Lottie. So if he left, she couldn't keep her grandmother in the house.

Which meant that he couldn't leave.

He fought back a spurt of panic. He'd find a solution, somehow. He wasn't stuck here forever. He just needed more time.

And he needed the truth—the whole truth—this time. Because something still wasn't right, his instincts warned him. Erin had only looked this anxious the past few days. She was hiding something even worse than Lottie's salary.

His jaw hardened. Independent or not, it was high time she came clean about her problems.

And she was going to do it tonight.

Erin stacked the last piece of leftover pizza in the plastic container, sealed the lid and set it inside the refrigerator. As she closed the door, she shot a wary glance at Wade.

He sat hunched over the table, his shoulders bulging beneath his black T-shirt as he nursed another beer. He'd grown edgier as the night wore on, his jaw rigid beneath his evening stubble, his brown eyes dark and brooding.

She walked back to the counter, her pulse tripping. He had something on his mind, all right. But there was no rushing Wade. He'd tell her when he was ready.

Until then, she'd work on her Thanksgiving menu. She opened the cupboard above the microwave and pulled out her recipe box. Then she grabbed her notepad and slid into the chair across from him at the table.

Their eyes met and the intensity in his gaze made her heart dip. She yanked her gaze away, then flipped blindly through her recipes, her pulse beating a tattered rhythm. That look didn't bode well. Whatever was on his mind apparently had to do with her.

"I talked to Lottie while you were giving your grandmother a bath," he said.

Oh, Lord. He'd found out about Lottie. She dragged her gaze back to his.

"Why didn't you tell me you had to pay her?" he demanded.

Because you'd feel obligated to stay. "I didn't think it would make much difference. There was nothing you could do. And once I get the bank loan, I can pay her with that."

"What about the house?"

"I don't know. I'll take it one repair at a time." And hope the blasted thing didn't collapse in the meantime.

He studied her for several hard seconds, the muscles in his face taut. "You realize I'm trying to help you."

"I know that."

"Then why don't you tell me the truth?"

"I am."

"Baloney. You've already lied about Lottie's paycheck. And there's more, isn't there?"

She bit her lip and his scowl deepened. "For God's sake, Erin. Do you think I'm blind? You hardly sleep. You're losing weight. You look like you're going to faint. And you avoid me. You say it wasn't that kiss—"

"It wasn't!"

"And Lottie says it isn't your grandma. So the problem has to be money."

She rubbed her arms. She never could fool Wade.

Grim lines bracketed his mouth. "You might as well tell me everything. I'll find out sooner or later. And I'd rather hear it from you."

He was right. There were no secrets in Millstown. Her students would tell their parents and they would tell everyone else. It was pointless to try to hide it.

Her long sigh filled the tense silence. "All right, fine. I found out on Monday that my contract won't be renewed."

His jaw slackened. "You got fired?"

"Not technically, but I'm finished after this semester."

"Because we were kissing?"

She spread her hands.

"Can they do that? Just because of a kiss?"

Because they were living together, but he didn't

need to know that. "It's a private school. I was on a temporary contract and I broke one of their rules. Apparently the parents complained."

He stood, strode to the sink and paced back. He stopped close to the table, his troubled gaze lowered to hers. "Erin, I'm sorry."

"It wasn't your fault."

"Of course it was."

"No, it wasn't." Nervous with him looming over her, she rose and walked to the counter. Then she turned and leaned back against it. "You told me to leave you alone. If I hadn't kept after you, that kiss never would have happened."

"That's ridiculous." He shot her an incredulous look. "Will you stop making excuses for me? I caused you to lose your job. You should yell at me or hit me, or something. I've messed up everything."

"No, you haven't." She sighed. "Look, so I lost my job. But it wasn't permanent anyway. It just ended sooner than I expected. And I've applied to substitute in the public schools again. The work might not be as steady, but I'll make enough to get by."

But not enough to pay off her debts. She pulled in an unsteady breath. Maybe it was time to give up teaching and look for a different job. But then she'd have less time with Grandma.

He stalked closer, his gaze hard on hers. "So, if it's no big deal, then why have you been so tense?"

Why indeed? She gnawed her lip.

"You could try the truth," he said.

She didn't dare. She knew him too well. He'd act heroic at his own expense.

"Don't you trust me?"

She frowned. "You know I do."

"Are you afraid I can't manage money?"

"Of course not. You were better at math than I was. You just never did your homework."

His perceptive gaze narrowed on hers. "Then this isn't about me, is it? It's you. You're too damn stubborn to ever let anyone help you."

"What?" she gasped.

"Admit it. You want to help everyone else, but no one can help you back."

"That's absurd." She was protecting him.

"Is it? Saint Erin. Sacrificing it all for your grandmother. Volunteering to the extreme. Working yourself to exhaustion so you won't look the slightest bit weak."

"That's not true! I like—"

"Feeling superior? Is that it? Like you're better than everyone else?"

"Of course not." Her face burned. "How can you even suggest that?"

"Then why won't you let me help you?" He stepped forward and grasped her arms. "What are you afraid of? That you might come across as human?"

Human? She sputtered. How dare he waltz in here all solvent and accuse her of not being human? He wasn't drowning in debt with two old ladies to support.

"Fine," she snapped. "You want to know how human I am? I'll tell you. I've totally screwed up, Wade. I owe you money. I owe the bank money, and I've already missed several payments. I've maxed out four credit cards, and now I can't make those payments, either. And then there are the medical bills. The taxes. And this house! And I've got two old women depending on me for everything. And if all that weren't enough, I just got fired from my job."

Her chest heaved. Her heart thundered against her ribs. Her vision blurred through her tears. "So are you happy now?" she asked, her voice breaking. "Is that human enough for you?"

"Yeah, it's human." He moved nearer and gathered her into his arms.

She stood stiffly, her throat throbbing, still infuriated by his accusations. She wasn't trying to be a martyr. She had to be strong. Her grandmother depended on her.

But he cupped her head with his hand and urged her closer against him. And suddenly she didn't want to be strong anymore. She didn't want to carry everyone's burdens. She was weary, so damned weary of all the exhaustion and stress. Just once, she wanted someone to comfort her.

Giving in to temptation, she melted against him. She rested her cheek on his chest and felt the strong, slow pulse of his heart. He felt solid and warm. Safe. She wrapped her arms around his lean waist and finally let herself crumble.

She probably wasn't being fair. He had enough on his mind without burdening him with her problems, but it felt good to confide the truth. And he'd always been her white knight, fighting her battles, making her troubles fade away.

While he stroked her hair and rubbed her back, she closed her eyes and inhaled deeply. Lord, he felt nice. She didn't want to move, didn't want to think. She wanted to rest in his strong arms forever.

But reality finally returned and she reluctantly lifted her head. He brushed the tears from her cheeks with his thumbs, then lowered his mouth to hers.

His kiss was tender, comforting, intimate. The kiss of an old and dear friend. It was sure and gentle and strong, like Wade himself, and she sighed when it came to an end.

Their gazes met and warmth eased through her heart. Dear Wade. He'd always protected her, cared for her. He'd been her savior, her rock, for as long as she could remember.

And he was the sexiest man with those arresting, whiskey-brown eyes. That desperado stubble that shadowed his stubborn jaw. And that firm, sensual mouth that curved to the most wicked grin.

He tightened his arms and shifted, bringing her closer against his strong body. His very hard, masculine body.

She realized how close they were standing. His warm breath fanned her face. His muscled thighs pressed against hers.

And she wanted him to kiss her again. Not gently this time, and definitely not as a friend. Man to woman. Out of control. Just as he had Friday night.

His eyes narrowed and darkened and her breath stalled in her throat. She swayed closer and clutched his hard shoulders. Her pulse leaped when he slanted his head.

And then his lips caught hers, fusing, singeing, shocking in a hot, plundering kiss that shorted her brain and sizzled her nerves. Exhilarated, she tightened her arms on his neck and devoured him back.

He growled low in his throat and pulled her tighter against him. Then he shifted, changing the angle of the kiss, and ravaged her mouth with his tongue. A throbbing pulse built inside her, a craving that threatened to explode.

Needing to feel him, caress him, she slid her hands across his wide shoulders. Impatient, she yanked his T-shirt free from his jeans and stroked his heated back with her hands. It wasn't enough. She wanted his hands on her, too. She whimpered her frustration.

He dragged his mouth from hers and buried his face in her neck. She felt his heart ram against hers, heard the ragged gasps of his breath. His hands swept her back, her buttocks, sending thrills of desire rushing through her. She shivered, restless for more.

With a groan, he captured her mouth again. The earth tilted, then whirled crazily as she lost herself to the rapture. Wade. The man she'd loved forever. The only man who'd ever felt right.

He tried to pull back, but she clung to him, unable to bear the separation. His harsh breaths sawed in her ear.

"Wade," she pleaded. "Make love to me, please."

"Erin, no." His eyes turned fierce, his features taut. "I can't. I—"

"Please, Wade. I need you."

He rested his forehead on hers and gripped her waist, as if preparing to push her away. Desperate, she molded her body to his.

"Erin." His voice was tortured, rough. "You know I can't stay—"

She covered his mouth with her hand, knowing what

he wanted to say. He couldn't promise forever. "I don't care," she said. She'd settle for now because she knew in her heart this was right. "Just love me tonight."

"Yes," he rasped and crushed his mouth to hers.

Chapter Ten

Moonlight pooled through the dark bedroom like smoke lingering over a smoldering wildfire. Wade shut the door behind him and turned the bolt, his heated gaze locked on Erin. He didn't know how they'd made it upstairs. He was so damned aroused he'd nearly taken her on the kitchen counter.

But she deserved better than that. Better than him, his conscience prodded. Better than a man who'd take what she offered, then bolt. But whether or not he deserved her, at least he could give her a bed.

His gaze still holding hers, he strode to the bedside table and snapped on the lamp. The soft light flared through the room, sparking highlights in her fiery hair. He'd fantasized about her for far too long to make love to her in the darkness. And he wanted every image of the coming night engraved in his brain forever—her naked breasts and thighs, the desire in her eyes when he took her.

She met him halfway across the room. She wrapped her arms around his neck and pressed her sweet body to his, surrounding him with her heat. He hooked his hands around her waist and pulled her flush against him. Hot blood rushed hard to his groin.

Erin. His ideal woman. The star of his erotic dreams for years. He wondered if he was hallucinating now.

He slid his hand along her smooth jaw and tipped up her chin, then gazed into her wondrous eyes. Emotion crowded his chest—longing and need, along with something deeper, more intense. Something vital. As if without her, he'd never be whole.

But twelve years ago he'd surrendered to this need and wounded her badly. Would it end any differently now?

"Are you sure about this?" he whispered roughly.

"Absolutely." She gazed up at him with the same expression he'd seen in her eyes as a kid. Trust. Admiration. Respect.

A thick pressure spread through his chest. God, she was special. She'd never treated him like the others in Millstown. She'd always acted as if she saw something good in him, something worthwhile, a part of him no one else had acknowledged. Not even himself.

He swallowed hard. He knew he didn't deserve her. A better man would refuse her and keep her from wasting herself on him. But he couldn't deny her twelve years ago, and he sure as hell didn't have the strength to do it now.

Moving reverently, he covered her mouth with his.

He feasted on the forbidden taste of her lips and inhaled the seductive scent of her skin. He plunged his hand through her silky hair and angled his mouth down harder.

She tightened her arms around his neck, bringing her breasts against his chest, and his pulse hammered hard in his veins. His blood grew hot, his brain blurred at the rocketing sensations.

Then she moved even closer, settling herself between his thighs, and desire lashed straight to his groin. He groaned. He needed hot, naked skin. Her wet, sizzling warmth—tight and pulsing around him.

And he needed it now.

It had been like this at the river. The raw urgency. The catastrophic loss of control.

The agonized need to possess her. To mark every glorious inch of her body, straight through to her generous soul. To brand her so damn thoroughly that she would be forever his. Only his.

And to make her want him, crave him, as much as he needed her.

Grappling for patience, he gentled the kiss, then almost wished he hadn't. Her soft lips moved more provocatively over his now. Her sensuous fingers blazed heat up his neck. And each flick of her hot, swirling tongue goaded him closer to desperation.

Needing to touch her bare skin, he slid his hands under her sweater and stroked the silky heat of her back. His hands trembling, he released the clasp on her bra, then cupped her breasts in his palms. She was soft and lush. Sweet. Fuller than he remembered. More than he'd ever dreamed.

Their mouths still fused, he stroked the curves of her breasts and rubbed the pebbled tips of her nipples. Heat lashed him with a fury and he fought to stay in control.

His heart thundering, he tore his mouth from hers, then grasped the edge of her sweater. "I need to see you."

"Yes." She helped him tug it over her head and dropped it, with her bra, to the floor.

His gaze lowered to her chest and his breath stalled in his throat. Her breasts were perfect—heavy and full, with tempting, pink-tinged nipples. Mesmerized, he traced the glorious curves with his hands, memorizing the play of light and shadow against her pale skin, the way her nipples begged for his kiss.

Hardly breathing, he bent and laved her breasts with his tongue. He tasted the heat, felt her hunger. Smelled the exotic scent of her skin. Heard her gasp as she clenched his shoulders.

His pulse ragged, his blood heavy, he captured her mouth in a kiss, showing her with his tongue what his body urged him to do. Desire overloaded his mind, driving out everything except the heavy throb in his groin. The need for Erin, naked, her bare skin slick against his.

With effort, he pulled away. His breathing rough, he reached over his shoulder and ripped off his T-shirt while she undid the snap on her jeans. She kicked them aside, then shook her hair from her shoulders.

His throat clogged. His gaze traveled from her full, naked breasts to the feminine curve of her waist, down long, firm legs and back to her thighs.

And suddenly he couldn't remember why this was wrong anymore.

She hooked her thumbs in the waistband of her panties. "Stop," he groaned, and she paused.

He slowly stalked forward, then stopped. His throat tight, his gaze still locked on hers, he settled his hands on her hips. "Let me," he urged. "I've fantasized about this for years."

Her eyes darkened and softened. Her lips parted with an uneven sigh. And she lifted her hands to his shoulders.

Still holding her gaze, he slipped his fingers under the waistband of the panties, and down through the thick thatch of hair. He found her slick, full nub and slowly stroked it.

She inhaled sharply and the tiny sound ripped straight to his heart. "Wade," she gasped.

"Look at me," he said, and she returned her gaze to his. Twelve years disappeared in that instant, and he saw the same stark need in her eyes. The same longing and passion and trust.

His entire body trembled.

Her breathing came in gasps. She clutched his shoulders, her nails scoring his flesh. His own pulse surged in his chest.

He moved fractionally closer, then slid his other hand to her buttocks. He kneaded and squeezed, and watched her lips part, her eyes close.

"Do you like this?" he rasped.

"Yes. Oh, yes." She opened her eyes. They were dark and dazed, and clouded with pleasure. He listened to her breathing rush, her gentle moans as he stroked her. His own desire surged in his veins.

Along with immense satisfaction. She wanted him. Wade Winslow. Only him.

"Wade, I…"

"Show me, Erin. Show me how much you want me." He slid his fingers over her with long, slow strokes. "Show me how much you need me."

She moved against him impatiently, but he deliberately decreased the tempo. He slowly brushed and rubbed the sensitized skin, dragging it out to heighten the pleasure.

"Wade!" Her gaze turned urgent, frantic. And then her face crumpled and she let out the high, keening cry that had haunted his dreams for years.

His heart swelled. She was beautiful. More than he ever remembered. More than he'd imagined. And she was his. Forever his. Hunger incinerated his brain.

He hauled her into his arms, then ground his mouth against hers in a hot, wild kiss that blasted his self-control. And suddenly he couldn't wait anymore. With one hand, he ripped off her panties and then carted her to the bed.

He dropped her onto the mattress but she clung to his neck. "Wait," he muttered. "My jeans."

She quickly rose to her knees. "Let me do it."

"No, I can't last—" He inhaled as she stroked his hard length through his jeans and gently undid the top button. Then she carefully lowered the zipper and his breath hissed out. He was pulsing with need, and when she caressed him, he nearly lost it.

"Erin. Oh, Erin." He tipped back his head and groaned as she stroked him to the edge of madness. Shaking, so far gone he couldn't think straight, he fisted his hands in her hair.

"Stop. I can't—" He jerked away, his entire body convulsing.

Desperate now, he shoved aside his pants and tackled her to the bed. Knowing he couldn't stand another touch, he grabbed her wrists with one hand and pinned them above her head. Then he slid his other hand over her flat stomach to the ripe, moist flesh between her thighs.

The scent of her first climax filled his head. Only the need to satisfy her completely kept him from losing control. With supreme effort, he beat back the desire twisting his guts. Then he stroked her repeatedly, relentlessly, bringing her back to the edge, until she trembled and called out his name. Until they both teetered on the border of madness.

He dropped her wrists, quickly protected himself, and rose between her thighs. Her face was flushed and contorted. Her nipples stood taut in her breasts, her whole body bared to his gaze. Open. Intimate. *Trusting.* He'd never seen anything so erotic in his life.

Erin. His woman. He'd been her first lover. He wanted to be her last. He wanted to fill her, mark her, make love to her so completely that she'd never look at another man.

"Wade—" She shuddered.

"Look at me," he commanded, poised above her.

Her blurred gaze met his. She looked dazed, mindless with passion. He needed her. Erin. Always Erin.

He drove into her in one strong thrust. Pleasure jolted through him, so staggering that he groaned. She was hot and wet and tight. So damned tight...

And he was beyond control. He couldn't think, couldn't stop. He could only plunge recklessly on, driven by desperation.

She convulsed around him. He saw the delirium in her eyes, the surrender, and knew she belonged to him. Only him. He wanted it to be forever.

"Erin," he cried. "Oh, Erin." And then his body exploded.

Hours later Wade stroked lazy circles on Erin's back. She lay flat on her stomach, her hair tangled wildly against the only pillow remaining on the bed, the edge of the sheet twisted over her ankles. Sometime during the night, they'd managed to get under the covers. Not that it mattered. The sheets, damp from their lovemaking, had eventually slid off the bed, joining the pillows and quilt on the floor.

He grinned, feeling a huge surge of contentment. She'd been insatiable. Demanding. He'd never had such mind-boggling sex in his life.

But they'd shared more than sex, and he knew it. His chest tight, his forehead furrowed, he fingered a strand of her hair. There was a connection between them, something he'd never felt with anyone else.

He frowned at the thickness clogging his throat and the unfamiliar flood of emotions. Erin had been his friend since childhood. But his smokejumping bros were his friends, too. They were fun and dependable, and he would give up his life to save them. But he'd kill anyone who threatened Erin. Even the thought of another man touching her filled him with rage.

But she wasn't just a sex partner, either. He'd never felt this possessiveness with a woman before, this overwhelming need to protect her.

Except that night at the river.

An ache tightened his chest, a wish that he could please her. If only he could give her what she needed, what she deserved. Commitment. But he wasn't a forever type of man. He was too restless, too easily bored to live in Millstown. And he sure as hell couldn't change his past.

Unease gripped his heart. He'd been selfish tonight. Damned selfish. And now he would pay the price.

He gazed at her naked back and the seductive curve of her hips. But selfish or not, he'd wanted her. Hell, he still did.

Resigned, he rose to his knees, slipped his hands under her breasts and stroked her. He felt her nipples harden in his palms, heard her breathing quicken. When he smoothed her hair from her neck and brushed a kiss across her nape, she moaned.

His blood heavy, he lifted her hips and spread her legs with his knees. Kneeling behind her, he teased her with his fingers until her body wept in his palm. His own desire rose with an urgency that stunned him. He'd never get enough of this woman. Never. How could he put a lifetime of need in one night? He entered her and they both groaned.

Maybe he couldn't give her forever. But he could give her what she wanted, at least tonight.

And make damned sure she remembered him when he was gone.

Early morning sunlight slanted through the windows when Erin opened her blurry eyes. She felt disoriented and depleted. Boneless.

She lay on her back with Wade's heavy arm draped over her stomach, pinning her to the mattress. As if she had the strength to move. Satiated, she ran her fingers along his huge, calloused hand, and traced the trail of scars up his arm.

He shifted and slid his hand to her breast, sending thrills through her tired body. Aftershocks from sensational sex, she thought with a smile. She'd never known a man could be so versatile, or that she could respond so intensely.

And oh, what a night. She turned her head to see his face. He was lying on his stomach, facing her, his pillow gone, his breathing heavy with sleep.

Her heart rolled over as she studied him. He was a gorgeous man with that thick, dark hair and rugged, masculine face. She reached out and stroked the stubble along his hard jaw. How could anyone look so devastating in the morning?

She caressed his bulging shoulders, his massive biceps. He was impressively strong, yet amazingly gentle, at least when he wanted to be. Her face warmed as she recalled a few of his rougher moments.

Her gaze returned to his face and a hard lump formed in her throat. Lord, she loved this man. Loved him with a yearning that shattered her soul. No one else had ever come close.

And she now knew no one ever would.

Despair tightened her chest. She couldn't fool herself any longer. She'd loved Wade since she was nine years old. Ever since he'd entered her life, he'd held her heart in his fist. Last night had only confirmed it.

But nothing had changed. He would eventually leave Millstown again. But this time would be worse, so much worse. Dear Lord, she'd never survive it.

He opened his eyes then and his whiskey-brown gaze met hers. Her pulse lurched and, despite her churning emotions, she felt the familiar rush of hunger. The flash of heat in his eyes warmed her soul.

Maybe he didn't want her love, but he wanted her body. And for now, it would be enough.

He hardened against her leg and in one quick movement pulled her beneath him. He raked his mouth over her nipple, sending pleasure shimmering through her nerves. She shivered and clutched his head.

Suddenly he looked up, and his raw gaze burned into hers. His jaw was rigid, his features taut, his attention focused only on her.

"You know you're going to kill me," he muttered.

"Me? What did I do?" Aroused now, she shifted beneath him. She wanted to feel him inside her, moving with relentless, powerful strokes. She wanted to abandon herself to the pleasure and to feel that glorious moment when he lost all control.

"You're a witch," he growled, thrusting into her.

She moaned at the delicious sensations cascading through her body. The huge, hard feel of Wade. The muscles bunching beneath her hands. The rapture of being held in his arms.

"Look at me," he said. Lost in the exhilaration, she pulled her gaze to his. His eyes were hard and narrow, his gaze intense.

Love surged inside her, an excruciating longing that shredded her heart. Words crowded her throat, but she choked them back. She couldn't tell him that she loved him. She could only take what he was willing to offer—this moment. She would seize it and build memories that would last forever. And try not to think about the end.

Chapter Eleven

Erin was still trying not to dwell on the future as she entered the sunroom the next afternoon, but Wade's lovemaking had shattered any hopes she had of protecting her heart. He'd stripped away her barriers, exposing longings she'd buried for years. She ached for him to stay with her in Millstown.

The aluminum extension ladder rattled and clanged against the sunroom windows, calling her attention outside. Wade came down from the roof, his work boots sure on the metal rungs. Her gaze traveled up his faded jeans to the tool belt slung over his hips and her breath jammed in her throat.

She shook her head in derision. It was pathetic when the sight of his legs sent her heart into spasms. But oh, what a body. And he certainly knew how to use it. Shivers ran through her nerves at the memories. His muscles bunching under her palms. His hard shoulders glistening with sweat. His hot mouth driving her to ecstasy time after time.

She sucked in a ragged breath. She was a mess, all right, and she needed to get a grip on her emotions. No matter how fabulous the sex was, Wade wouldn't stay in Millstown. And it would hurt even worse if she let herself hope.

He pulled off his leather work gloves when he reached the ground. Still trying to rein in her fantasies, she watched him stride across the lawn to the four teens trimming bushes along the driveway. His loose-hipped swagger dried her throat.

The buzz of hedge trimmers cut off abruptly at his approach. He stopped next to the bushes and braced his hands on his hips. Even from a distance, his low voice quickened her pulse. She shook her head and grasped at control. She definitely needed to rein in her emotions.

But then Jay set down his trimmer and planted his hands on his hips, imitating Wade's posture, and her composure slipped even more. Did Wade have any idea how much those kids idolized him? What a role model he'd become? How desperately they needed him to guide them?

The muscles along her chest squeezed tight and she beat back a strong surge of yearning. Wade was the best thing that had ever happened to those kids—and to her—but she had to face reality. He had his own plans, which didn't include staying in Millstown. And no matter what he did, she had to get on with her life—which at the moment meant inviting the boys to Thanksgiving dinner.

She crossed to the sunroom door. Wade gestured to the house just then and Sean turned in her direction. She caught sight of his face and froze with her hand on the door. Dear Lord. What had happened? His left eye was swollen shut. His upper lip had split open and a raw welt discolored his cheek.

His father. She tightened her grip on the door. They'd suspected him of abuse before, but Sean's mother had always denied it. And no one had the guts to press charges.

Her anger rising, she swung open the door. Well, she didn't cower to anyone. She was going to find out exactly what happened, and notify the police. That creep wouldn't get away with beating Sean this time.

Her face burning, she marched down the back steps and across the lawn to the driveway, her outrage swelling with every step. If there was one thing she couldn't tolerate, it was a bully. And it was time that man paid for his crimes.

Wade turned as she neared the group. "Be right back," he said to the boys. He strode forward and cut her off.

She stepped to the side, but he moved the same way and blocked her. "Excuse me," she said, stepping sideways again. "I need to talk—"

"Later." He grasped her arm and swung her back towards the house.

"But I need to—"

"In a minute." He dragged her around the lilac bushes to the side of the house. Then he released her arm.

She huffed out her breath. "What's wrong with you? I only want to talk—"

"Forget it. I'm handling it."

"Handling what?"

"Sean. Isn't that what you're all fired up about?"

She crossed her arms. Of course Wade knew what had happened. He'd had plenty of bruises himself before his father went to prison.

"His father's done this before," she said. "We need to call the police and arrest him."

"I said to forget it."

"But—"

"Look, Erin. Sean won't admit anything. He's too scared right now. And humiliated. If you call in the authorities, he'll just deny it, and his old man will hurt him more."

"Then what do you suggest? That we ignore it?"

A hard glint shone in his eyes. "I didn't say that."

She knew that look. A sick dread churned through her gut. "You're not going out there."

"Not until the kid's safe," he agreed flatly.

"You're not going out there at all. What if the guy has a gun?" Panic crawled up her chest. "Promise me. You're not—"

"Sean can stay here, right?"

"Of course, but—"

"But nothing. I'm handling this," he warned. "I mean it. Just keep Sean here. And don't call anyone until I get back."

She saw the rigid line of his jaw, the cold fury in his eyes—not for her, but men who bullied their kids. And she knew she couldn't stop him. Wade never had followed the rules.

"Trust me," he urged.

Her heart softened. He'd lived Sean's life. He'd know better than anyone how to handle Sean's father. There was no one she would trust more. "You'll be careful?"

His eyes warmed. "Yeah."

She lifted her hands in surrender. "Fine. I'll stay out of it. But can I at least invite the kids for Thanksgiving dinner?"

"Sure." He slung his arm around her shoulder and maneuvered her back toward the yard. He grinned down at her then, and sexy grooves bracketed his mouth. Her gaze traveled from his lips to his eyes and desire splintered through her, a need so strong that she gasped.

He stopped abruptly, his heated gaze locked on hers. She saw the hunger in his eyes, felt the familiar tension rise between them.

And then he hauled her into his arms. Her heart sped at the feel of his hands on her back, the hard warmth surrounding her body.

"I've been wanting to do this all day," he said, his voice gruff. She thrilled when he lowered his head. Shivered as his warm lips touched hers. And then lost herself to the moment.

His mouth slanted hard over hers, sparking tremors along her skin and tumbling her heart through her chest. He cradled her chin with his rough hand, devouring her mouth with his tongue. Plundering deeply, driving harder, until her body jolted with pleasure. Until urgency sizzled her nerves.

She clung to his neck, her muscles trembling. Desire burned in her veins. She yearned for him, ached for him. She wanted to climb right into his skin.

When he lifted his head, she moaned at the loss. "Don't stop. Oh, please don't stop." She pressed herself to his lower body.

"Erin," he groaned. "You're making me crazy." He tugged her head to his chest and pulled her flush against him. He pressed his hand to her lower back to hold her still. "Don't move," he ordered.

She wrapped her arms around his waist, then squeezed her eyes shut and dragged in air. His heart raced against her cheek. His muscular body shuddered against hers. She could feel every inch of his arousal and her own body wept in response.

Still quivering with need, she held on to him, absorbing his strength, his smell, his warmth. It wasn't enough, not nearly enough, and she whimpered her frustration.

Long moments later, when the burning finally eased to an ache, she raised her head. Her gaze met his and she saw matching heat in his eyes. Desire and something more. Longing. *Love?* Her heart lurched to a halt.

And then he pulled her head to his chest again and buried his face in her hair. Her heart full, her mind racing, she tightened her hold on his waist and hugged him back.

Dear Lord. Did Wade love her? Was it possible? Or had she only imagined that look?

He'd never told her that he loved her. But maybe he didn't want to admit it, or didn't want her to know.

Or maybe she was mistaking his lust for love, just as she had before. Unless she hadn't misunderstood back then...

Her heart trembled. She wouldn't think about it. She

didn't dare set herself up for more heartbreak. And she certainly wouldn't ask him how he felt. He might panic and bolt.

But for the first time, she felt a flicker of hope.

After a moment he stepped back, but looped one arm over her shoulder, as if unwilling to break the contact. Her heart nearly bursting, she searched his eyes, but all she saw was hunger. Whatever emotion he'd felt, he'd hidden behind the safety of lust.

The teens were grinning when they joined the group, and her face warmed at their snickers. She'd forgotten about their audience. "Thanks a lot," she muttered.

He squeezed her shoulder and the heat in his eyes made her pulse trip. At least the kiss had frustrated him, too.

She inhaled to compose herself. "Hey, guys," she said. "I wanted to invite you all for Thanksgiving dinner Thursday if your families don't have anything planned. I bought a huge turkey, so there'll be lots of food. Way too much for just us, so I'd really like you to come."

The boys shuffled their feet, their expressions suddenly blank, and she frowned. What teenage boy turned down food? And from the little she knew about their backgrounds, she doubted they had other plans.

"I figure we'll eat around three, but you can come anytime before that. You don't have to let me know in advance," she added when they still didn't answer. "Just show up if you can."

No one met her gaze and she looked at Wade, perplexed. He motioned with his head, so she started back across the parched grass to the sunroom. Maybe he'd figure out what was wrong.

"The dinner's no big deal," she heard him say when she entered the sunroom. "You don't have to wear fancy clothes. We'll just eat turkey and mashed potatoes and watch the game."

She blinked. So that was the problem. They were afraid that the dinner was formal. But it made sense. To a kid from Newburg Village, Mills Ferry probably seemed like the White House.

And Wade had sensed the problem. Because he'd been like them once. A thick knot formed in her chest.

"I'll come," Jay said. The other boys murmured agreement.

"Good." Wade said. "Now, listen. I need to finish early today. Go ahead and load those clippings on the truck. I'll haul them to the dump before I drop Lottie off at the airport. Sean, you can give me a hand with the ladder."

Erin ducked behind a chair as they walked toward the sunroom. "Steady that end as I bring it down," Wade said. Seconds later she heard a metallic clank.

"I've got a favor to ask you," Wade said.

"Me?" Sean sounded surprised.

"Yeah. You have this week off from school, right?"

"Yeah, sort of."

She grimaced. Nothing like encouraging a kid to play hooky. But Sean probably wouldn't go to school with his face battered, anyway. And she could call and get his homework.

"I wondered if you could stay here for a while, starting tonight. You know, just live out here while Lottie's in Florida. I don't want to leave Erin alone with her grandmother."

"Where are you going?"

"Nowhere, but I've got to clean out Norm's duplex this week, so I won't always be in the house. I need somebody who can just hang around, be available in case Erin needs help. Like if her grandmother falls."

Sean didn't answer. The ladder clanked in the silence.

"I'll stop by your house on my way back from the airport and pick up whatever you need," Wade added.

"But then he'll know where I am," Sean blurted. "And he'll…he'll…"

Erin's stomach wrenched.

"I'll deal with him," Wade said. "Don't worry. I won't let anything happen to you."

She sank to the floor, her throat tight.

"You're safe now," Wade said gently. "I promise. I always take care of my friends."

"Okay," Sean said, his voice quivering.

"Good. And you might let Erin take a look at that face. Now let's get this ladder into the shed."

Erin huddled beside the chair, her stomach raw, her throat aching, and squeezed back a hot rush of tears. He'd handled that perfectly. *Perfectly.* Oh, Lord. He was so amazingly good for those kids.

And for her.

She pressed her face to her knees, rocking back and forth, feeling totally shredded inside. She loved that man, wanted him so much that it shattered her heart. And unless she'd imagined that look in his eyes, he loved her, too.

The solution should be so simple. For all their sakes, he should stay.

She lifted her head and slowly massaged her temples. Finally she heaved out a sigh. The answer seemed simple, all right, but nothing was ever easy when it came to Wade Winslow.

Especially convincing him that he belonged in Millstown.

Wade pulled his truck alongside the curb in front of Sean's trailer late that evening and cut the engine. The trailer squatted on a cramped, weedy lot in Newburg Village, flanked by patches of dirt and discarded beer cans. A tattered awning sagged listlessly over the door, as if it lacked the strength to collapse.

He pushed open the cab door and climbed out. The frantic, high-pitched barking of a dog warned the neighborhood of his arrival. A man shouted, the dog squealed and the barking abruptly stopped. The canned laughter of a television sitcom filled the silence.

His gut hardened. Newburg Village. The place where he'd grown up. A different trailer occupied his old space now, but the same indifference pervaded the park, the same poverty and despair.

His jaw tightened and he brushed the old feelings aside. He hadn't come here to reminisce about his childhood. He'd come to convince Sean's father to leave him alone. And he intended to do it fast.

He tramped through the dry weeds to the trailer, climbed the bowed metal step and knocked on the door. When no one answered, he pounded again.

Growing impatient, he glanced around. The curtain in the next trailer moved, and he scowled. Too bad those neighbors hadn't been so nosy when Gill was beating his kid.

Disgusted, he turned back and banged on the door. He knew Gill was in there. Light from his television flickered through the slits in the shade. So why the hell didn't he answer? "Hey, Gill!" he shouted. "Open up."

Nothing happened. But damned if he was giving up. Frustrated, he yanked open the door.

The familiar stench of whiskey stopped him cold. And suddenly he was ten years old again, coming home from school. Scared he'd find his old man waiting to beat him. Terrified to walk through the door.

His pulse drummed in his ears. His breath turned shallow and fast. Raw fear crept down his spine.

Then he scrubbed a hand over his face. Hell. He didn't have time to relive that crap. He had to take care of Sean.

"Gill," he called again. "You in there?"

"Yeah."

Shaking off the old dread, he stepped inside the trailer, then reached along the wall and flicked on the light. His gaze swept the dirty dishes on the kitchen table, the clothes scattered across the floor, to the man sprawled in a recliner by the television set. The chair slowly swiveled to face him.

Gill was a brawny, balding man in his early forties, with mean eyes glazed from whiskey. Wade pictured those powerful arms hitting Sean, and fury hardened his gut. He was going to nail this bastard. He'd never get his hands on Sean again.

Gill's eyes slitted. "Who the hell are you?"

"Wade Winslow."

Gill held his gaze for a moment, then lifted his glass to his mouth and drained it. His eyes returned to Wade. "I knew your old man. You look like him."

"So I hear." Disgust washed through him at the reminder of his father. His heritage. Where he came from and what he was. He shoved the feeling aside. "I'm here to talk about Sean."

"What about him?"

Wade planted his hands on his hips. "He's living with me now. And I'm warning you to leave him alone."

Gill stood. He was short, about five-nine, with the meaty fists of a brawler. "You telling me what to do with my kid?"

"He's not your kid anymore. He's mine. There'll be a hearing to make it legal. And you're going to sign him away.

"But in the meantime, you don't go near him. You don't talk to him. You don't look at him. You don't even breathe in his direction. In fact, you forget he ever existed.

"You do it my way and I won't press charges," he continued, his voice flat. "You contact him again, and I'll have you nailed to the wall."

"Is this some sort of joke?"

His jaw stiffened. "Child abuse doesn't amuse me."

Gill sauntered to the kitchen counter. He uncapped a bottle of whiskey, splashed some into his glass and took a long slug. Then he wiped his mouth with the back of his hand. "A man's got a right to discipline his kid."

"A *man* doesn't bully a helpless boy."

Gill stilled. "You saying I'm not a man?"

Wade thought of Norm, the best man he'd ever known. "Hell, you don't even come close."

Gill slowly set down the glass.

The hairs prickled on the back of Wade's neck. A vision of Sean, his face battered, flashed through his mind. This man was scum. He deserved to be taken down.

He deliberately widened his stance.

A heartbeat later, Gill charged. Wade slipped to the right and Gill barreled past. He crashed against the door, staggered back, then recovered and whirled around. His breath came in heavy gasps.

And a switchblade appeared in his hand.

Awareness slinked down Wade's spine and he tensed. Gill intended to use that knife. That certainty lodged hard in his gut.

For an eternity, neither man moved. The television blared in the background. The smell of whiskey permeated the air. Wade's vision narrowed on Gill, every nerve poised to react.

Gill circled around him, his eyes deadly, his smile feral. Wade moved with him, battling the adrenaline rising inside him, the primitive urge to attack. His instincts told him to wait, to have patience. To think.

When his back was to the sink again, Gill lunged. Wade dodged right to escape the knife, then whirled and dove for his wrist. His momentum sent them sprawling against the counter, with him on top.

Gill tried to shake him off, but he hung on. They toppled sideways, turned and smashed through a chair to the floor. The table tipped and dishes crashed around them.

Wade instantly pinned him down amid the wreckage, keeping a death grip on his wrist. Sweat ran into his eyes as he fought to force the knife from his hand.

Gill surged against him. Wade shifted one knee to his chest for better leverage and grappled for control of the knife. His biceps bulging, his heart hammering, he slammed Gill's wrist to the floor. The stench of sweat filled his nostrils. Harsh grunts punctuated the air.

Gill's grip finally slackened and the knife clattered free. Still holding him down, Wade gasped for breath.

Satisfaction surged through him. He had him. And now he'd show this swine how Sean felt. He raised his fist, poised to bash Gill's face to a pulp.

Just like his old man had done to him.

And suddenly, before he could block them, the memories came crashing back and he was pinned to the floor. His father's dank breath reeked down on him. His mottled face loomed overhead. His heavy weight crushed him as he raised his fist to his face.

Panic raced through his nerves. Raw fear slammed through his throat. He bucked, battling for freedom, but he couldn't dislodge the man's weight. "Dad, don't," he'd pleaded. Hysteria clawed through his gut. "Please, don't—"

The fist slammed into his jaw. Fierce pain shot through his face. Blinding, excruciating pain, and he screamed.

He struggled to twist away, to dodge the blows, but he was too small and couldn't budge. He felt helpless, weak. Trapped.

His terror rose. "Please don't," he whimpered. Nausea swirled through his gut. "Please, I—"

The fist smashed into his nose, and an agony of pain

blasted through him. Blood spurted from his face. His dazed whimpers mingled with his pleading sobs.

He couldn't stop him. He couldn't get away. And begging only fueled the man's rage.

Hell. Wade blinked. His heart slammed against his rib cage. His pulse thundered through his skull.

And he realized that he couldn't do it. Damn, but he couldn't do it. No matter how much Gill deserved it, no matter how badly as he longed for revenge, he couldn't lower himself to that level.

Frustrated, he lowered his arm. "The police will have all the proof they need," he promised. "Pictures. Statements. You stay away from Sean, and I'll leave you alone. But you even look at him again and you'll go to prison." He wrenched his knee against Gill's chest.

Gill grunted. He stank of whiskey and sweat.

"Where's his mother?" Wade demanded.

"Gone."

"Since when?"

"Two, three months back. I don't know."

That figured. She'd saved herself but abandoned her kid. But he'd let the authorities worry about that complication. He just wanted to keep Sean safe. "You'll get the restraining order tomorrow. Be here."

He shifted his weight off Gill and rose. "You got that?" His pulse still thundering, he pocketed the switchblade.

"Yeah." Gill sat up and rubbed his wrist. "The brat's yours."

His gut tightened. Another heart-rending display of fatherly love.

Disgusted, he crossed to the door and walked out, letting the door bang shut behind him. The cool air dried the sweat on his face as he limped back through the weeds to his truck.

He jerked open the cab door, then paused and sucked in a breath. And for a long moment he just looked at the neighborhood and let himself remember the past. The hunger. The violence. The father who'd made him who he was.

But maybe not completely.

He looked back at Sean's trailer cowering amid the trash. Why hadn't he hit Gill? He'd wanted to. Hell, he'd ached to slam his fist in that face.

But he'd controlled himself. Unlike his father, he hadn't acted on impulse. Not this time. Not when it had mattered.

A huge sense of release surged through him. He hadn't turned into his father. Despite his sordid childhood, he wasn't chained to his past.

Thanks to Norm.

The realization floored him, but it was true. Norm had made him the man he was, not his father. He was more like Norm than he'd thought.

He really was Norm's son.

Feeling lighter suddenly, freer, as if he'd loosened a weight from his back, he climbed into the truck and started the engine. Norm would have been damned proud of him tonight. He'd controlled himself. He'd gotten Sean. He'd saved a kid from a hopeless life.

His hand froze on the gearshift. Now what was he going to do with him?

Chapter Twelve

So what was he going to do with Sean? Wade still hadn't answered that question three days later as he followed the kid up the stairs into the turret off Erin's third floor.

"Wow," Sean breathed. He stopped inside the large, high-ceilinged room ringed with windows and gawked.

Wade smiled. He'd reacted the same way the first time he'd seen the turret. Erin had led him up the winding stairs, her red braids swinging against her back. Both the girl and the house had awed him.

He limped to the window, slipped his hands into the back pockets of his jeans and gazed out at the view. Below the mill, the Potomac River wound sluggishly through the bare trees, its water low on the banks. To the west, a steep canyon led to a high mountain ridge speckled with pine trees and granite.

Behind him, Sean rushed around the room and peered out the windows. "Hey, Wade?" The tremor in his voice caught his attention.

"Yeah?" He turned. The bruise around Sean's eye appeared yellow in the morning light. Small scabs still dotted his lips.

"Do you think Erin would let me use this room? I mean, if she doesn't need it for anything else."

"You want to turn it into your bedroom?"

Sean shoved his hands into his pockets and hunched his shoulders. "Maybe. Nah. It's probably a dumb idea."

"Oh, I don't know." He glanced around. "This would make a great bedroom."

"Really?" Sean's gaze flew to his.

"We'd need to make some repairs, though."

"Like what?"

"Well, we'd have to make sure the roof holds. You wouldn't want rain coming in on you during the night." If the drought ever ended. "And patch the damaged ceiling." He held his hand to the window and felt the cold air puff through. "Caulk the windows. Replace the sills that have rotted out. Make sure the heat works up here." He exhaled. Close off the fireplace. Sand and varnish the floor, paint the walls...

"I can help." Sean's eyes pleaded with his. "I don't have anything else to do."

"You mean, like homework?"

Sean grimaced and Wade's mouth tugged up in sympathy. He'd rarely done his homework, either, except when Rose had insisted. "We'll see what Erin says."

But guilt slid into his gut, clamping down hard on

his conscience. He shouldn't be starting projects when he wouldn't be here to complete them. Or let Sean get the wrong idea and think he was going to stay.

He crossed his arms, knowing he had to deal with this problem. He could stay in Maryland for a few months, but he had to report for refresher training in the spring. And once the fire season started, he'd be working nonstop. He wouldn't have time for a kid.

Erin would let Sean stay here. No doubt, she'd apply for permanent custody, and the court would have to agree. The McCuens had power in this town. And he could send her money to support him.

But it wasn't enough. Erin was a great woman, but Sean needed a man to guide him. He'd learned that lesson from Norm.

And no way could he be that man.

He frowned down at the river. He'd gotten himself into a mess, all right, and he had no idea how to solve it.

"So here you are." Erin entered the room, snapping him back to the present. Her face was flushed and wisps of loose hair clung to her neck.

His gaze traveled over her full breasts to the seductive swing of her hips, and his libido predictably stirred. "We were looking over the turret," he said. "Thinking maybe we'd make this Sean's bedroom, if it's all right with you."

Sean turned and pressed his face to the window, as if fascinated by the view.

"Well, I don't know. I never thought about it." She glanced around the room, then lifted her gaze to his. "What do you think?"

His heart rolled. He thought he could get lost in those eyes. They were the most amazing shade of green, like the Bitterroot Forest at twilight. "We'd have to repair a few things first."

Sean spun around. "I can help."

Erin shrugged. "It's fine with me. As long as Wade says it's safe."

He looked at Sean. "Why don't you run down and get a tape measure and something to write with? We'll make a list of what we need."

"Okay!" Sean bolted from the room, his footsteps loud on the stairs. Wade stalked over to Erin. Her face was still pink, her lips parted slightly. The heat in her eyes made his heart kick.

"You're breathing fast," he said, his voice thick. He ran his gaze down her body. "I hadn't noticed you were that out of shape."

"I'm not. I'm just exhausted." Her lips curved. "I'm not getting much sleep these days."

And he knew why. Images swamped his mind—of her bare breasts, the nipples tight with arousal. Her neck arched back, her hair pooling over the pillow. Her pale thighs parted, beckoning him to her heat.

He locked his hands on her waist and tugged her close, fitting her against his erection. Her gorgeous eyes darkened and she parted her lips with a sigh.

His pulse heavy, he moved his mouth over hers. His tongue slid along the silky depths, tasting, seeking. Invading. His blood thundered hard in his ears.

How could she affect him like this? One look, one touch, and his thoughts turned instantly carnal. And the need grew worse every day.

He cupped her head with his hand and delved deeper, intensifying the kiss. Her tongue twined with his, fanning him into urgency. He rocked his pelvis hard against hers.

She moaned. Her arms tightened around his neck, her breasts flattened against his chest. Her response made him even hotter.

He couldn't get enough of this woman. He craved her day and night. He'd never known anyone could fascinate him so much.

He slipped his hands to her bottom, then cupped and pulled her against him. She gasped against his mouth.

He wanted to crush her to him. Strip off her clothes and take her right now in the turret. Take her a million times, a million ways. On the floor. Against the wall. Above her. Below her. And brand her forever as his.

But the footsteps pounding the stairs caught his attention and he dragged his mouth from hers. Her eyes slowly opened. Her lids were heavy, her pupils glazed with desire.

"We've got company."

"Oh." Erin blinked, pulled back and straightened her sweater as the steps grew closer. Then she reached up to repair her hair and shot him a lopsided grin. "I guess this is the drawback of being a parent."

A parent. His breath froze and a sudden vision filled his mind. Of Erin, her belly distended, her full breasts laden with milk. Erin, pregnant with his child. Holding a dark-haired baby in her arms. *His son.*

A longing surged through him. A wild need that weakened his knees. A need to plant his seed in her and to bind her to him, body and soul. To make her forever his.

To have a family. Oh, God. His knees shook.

And raw panic surged through his gut. What was he thinking? What was he doing? He could never stay here with Erin.

Sean came into the room, carrying a tape measure and pad of paper, expectation bright on his face.

His nerves jumped. His pulse raced. He dragged in air and struggled to breathe. He couldn't have a wife. A family. A son. What the hell was he thinking?

He stepped back, feeling caged. He had to get out of here. He needed space. Time. Air.

Erin and Sean eyed him strangely. "Look," he said. "I, uh. I need to go. I'll, um, be back in a little while."

"But I thought we were making a list," Sean said.

He looked at Erin. Her eyes were huge. Knowing. Hurt. *Damn.* She knew exactly what was wrong, because she knew him so well.

Guilt flooded through him. He didn't want to hurt her. But that was exactly what would happen when he left. And it would be worse the longer he stayed.

Desperate now, he looked at Sean. "Why don't you measure the windowsills? I've got a few errands to run."

"But it's Thanksgiving," Sean said. "Everything's closed."

He saw the pain in Sean's eyes, the withdrawal. And felt disgusted for putting it there. How much worse would it be when he left?

Erin rested her hand on Sean's shoulder. "Wade has to take care of some last-minute things for me. I'll help you measure, then we can make a list of what you'd like to bring up here. You can figure out the repairs later on."

With guilt riding hard in his gut, he turned and strode out the door. He felt frustrated, angry. At Sean for expecting so much. At Erin, for bailing him out again. At himself for letting them down.

For acting like a coward and running away. Knowing full well that it wasn't going to help.

Because no matter how fast and far he moved, he couldn't outrun his heart.

He was right. The punishing ride on the Harley didn't solve a damned thing. He'd rolled open the V-Rod's throttle and taken the bike to the limit, tearing up the canyon past Mills Ferry, rocketing through the mountains into West Virginia and back.

But it hadn't done any good. The aggressive ride had wrung out his body, but not the harsh need gnawing his chest. Or the demons that told him he was wrong to hope, wrong to dream, wrong to imagine he could stay in Millstown.

And not just because it was Millstown. He pulled into a turnout along the ridge above town and idled the engine. Then he ripped off his helmet and gazed down at the tiny town. At the old brick houses and ancient trees. The streets, as narrow and unbending as the minds of the people who lived there.

And he struggled to be objective. Sure, some people despised him, and probably always would. But not everyone felt that way, he had to admit. And he could live with that.

So why did he still want to bolt? Was it because of his job? He loved smokejumping. The excitement of fighting fires, the danger. The sense of accomplishment and camaraderie. The mobility and constant change, the thrill of leaping from the plane. He'd go crazy working in an office.

But it wasn't that simple, either, and he had to face that harsh truth. There was something deeper that kept him from staying, a deficiency inside him. Something lacking. Something that fueled his need to escape.

The problem was him. Not the town, not the job. Just him. He could never be a family man. And he couldn't do a damn thing to change that. No matter how much he wanted to please Erin.

Feeling as if a rock had lodged in his gut, he yanked his helmet back over his head. Then he kicked the bike into gear and rumbled down the mountain back into Millstown.

The pulsing reverberations of the Harley announced his arrival at Mills Ferry minutes later. He pulled in beside Jay's rusted Ford and rocked the bike back on its kickstand.

And then castigated himself even more. The teens had arrived. He should have stayed to help Erin instead of leaving her to do the work.

But wouldn't it be like that when he was gone?

With unease roiling his gut, he climbed off his bike. His knee had stiffened up, which he probably deserved after taking off like that. Ignoring the pain, he limped around the house and up the porch.

The aroma of roasted turkey greeted him as he tramped through the door. Suddenly starving, he pulled off his leather gloves and jacket, and tossed them over the newel post.

He glanced into the parlor. Grandma sat in her chair,

showing her quilt blocks to Sean. The sight loosened the knot in his chest. Sean was a damned good kid, and he was amazingly patient with the old woman.

Erin's voice drifted from the dining room and he turned around, surprised. He'd expected to eat in the kitchen like they usually did. She must have opened the dining room up for the kids.

He slid back the pocket door and slipped inside. Erin stood in the center of the room, watching Jay and Alex insert a leaf in the table. They all looked up when he came in.

His gaze fastened on Erin's. Her eyes were wide, her expression concerned. For him. The lump in his gut instantly softened, replaced by a haze of warmth. No matter what else was wrong in his life, Erin always felt right.

"Hey, Wade," Jay said. The teen had cut his hair and removed his eyebrow ring for the occasion.

He nodded back. "Jay. Alex."

"Okay, guys," Erin announced. "You can bring in the other leaf now."

She walked over and put her hand on his arm as the two boys filed from the room. "Are you okay?" she asked, her voice low.

"Yeah. I'm sorry I cut out like that."

"That's okay."

"No, it's not. I should have stayed and helped you."

"I didn't need help. Listen, Wade." She glanced back at the door. "I just want you to know. What we have right now, it's, well, it's amazing. Special. And I don't want to spoil it."

"But—"

She pressed her hand to his lips. "But nothing. I'm not thinking about the future. Okay? Let's just enjoy the moment. Let's not worry about anything else."

He gazed into her wide, green eyes. Reached out and brushed his finger along her smooth jaw. She deserved far more than this moment. More than him.

His heart expanded with guilt and need, and a longing so deep that his gut ached. God, she was special. He wanted to hold her and never let go.

But Jay and Alex trudged through the door just then, each holding an end of the table leaf, and Erin stepped away. "Thanks, guys," she said. "Just pull this section loose and set the leaf in. Then you can bring in the table pads and put them on."

She walked over to the sideboard against the far wall. He followed her, regrets still pulling at his chest. He knew damn well she wasn't the type to live for the moment. But he had nothing else to offer.

She bent to paw through a drawer. Then she pulled out a tablecloth and handed it over. "We always use this on Thanksgiving. It looks a little wrinkled, though. Maybe I should iron it."

"It's fine." He draped it over the back of a chair. The boys traipsed past on their way to retrieve the table pads and Jay shot him a grin.

She knelt down in front of the cabinet and pulled a wooden box from the bottom shelf. The motion molded her jeans to her hips. "Here's the silverware." She held it out. "You can have the kids set the places."

He grabbed the box and grinned. She looked cute bossing him around. And he could think of some damned interesting ways to put that trait to use. But not with the kids milling around. "You think they know how?"

She pursed her lips. "You're probably right. I'll show them."

He set the box on top of the sideboard. The boys returned with the table pads and fitted them in place.

Erin handed him a plate. "This is for the olives and pickles. Just put it on the kitchen counter."

He turned the small dish over in his hands. The clear glass was divided into sections and trimmed with decorative bubbles. He ran his hand over the edge. The sensation dredged up a memory.

"My mother had a dish like this," he said, amazed that he remembered.

"Really?" She closed the cabinet and rose to her feet. "It's a Candlewick. They're collectibles now. Do you still have it?"

"No." Another memory crowded in. "My father threw it against the wall when they were arguing." And his mother cried when it smashed.

He didn't have anything from his past. Not like Erin. He glanced at the claw-footed table and the chandelier with crystal pendants. She had history. Traditions. Special tablecloths and dishes and silver. He only had memories, most of them bad.

The boys awkwardly spread the plaid cloth over the table. His gaze traveled to where one edge pooled on the floor. He frowned as another memory intruded. "Didn't there used to be a rug in here?" His gaze moved across the floor. The wood was darker under the table where the rug once sat. The sun had faded the rest.

And that wasn't the only change. Despite the ornate

molding and imposing chandelier, the room seemed emptier now. He tried to visualize how it had looked years ago. He strode to the far wall and noted the tell-tale change in the floor. "And there was a cabinet here, right?" He turned back to Erin.

"That's right."

"What happened to them?"

"I sold them." She turned and left the room.

Frowning, he followed her into the kitchen. "Why?"

"Money." She shrugged. "Antiques go for a lot these days."

Her nonchalance didn't fool him. This woman revered history, especially if it involved Mills Ferry. She wouldn't part with a family heirloom unless her situation was dire.

The muscles along his jaw tensed. She was desperate, all right, and he'd done damn little to help her.

And that bothered him. He was good at solving problems. He made a living doing exactly that. He leaped in, assessed a situation, and fixed it. He took charge and put out the fire.

And it was time he did that for Erin. Somehow he had to solve her financial problems. That way, no matter what happened in the future, at least she wouldn't be broke.

But how could he rescue her from bankruptcy? Wade mulled that over as he helped the teens demolish dinner. They'd consumed mountains of mashed potatoes and stuffing, and picked the turkey clean. Now they were making serious inroads into the vegetables.

Erin smiled from across the table. "I should have

mashed more potatoes. I can't believe how much food you guys eat."

He glanced around the table. "You think this is something, you should see smokejumpers coming in from a fire."

"You get hungry, huh?" Jay said.

"Yeah. No matter how much food you have, it never seems like enough. Sometimes, you even run out. I jumped a fire in Alaska once where that happened and things got pretty grim. There was even a fight."

Jay's eyes widened. "Over food?"

"Yeah." All eyes swiveled to his. "You do odd things when you're starving."

"I don't understand," Erin said, setting down her fork. "How can they expect you to work without food?"

"They don't. They give us plenty of food, even if it's mostly freeze-dried. But if it takes too long to get the fire out, and they're too busy to drop supplies..."

He shrugged and dug into his sweet potatoes. "This really is a great meal, though."

"It sure is," Sean said.

"Nice to see...such good appetites," Erin's grandmother chimed in. Her gaze settled on Jay. "Are you from the bank?"

Jay paused, his fork halfway to his mouth. "The bank?"

"This is Jay, Grandma," Erin said patiently. "He's helping Wade clean up the yard. Remember? They trimmed back your roses like you wanted. You're going to have some wonderful flowers this year."

Grandma leaned forward. Her hand trembled on the table. "Stealing my money. They think I don't know."

"Grandma doesn't trust the bank," Erin explained, rolling her eyes.

The boys gaped at Grandma for several seconds, then returned their attention to their food. Wade supposed they'd seen enough deviant behavior in their lives to take an odd delusion in stride.

He broke off a piece of roll and slathered it with butter. Grandma's fixation with the bank intrigued him, though. What money did she think they were stealing? The family was flat out broke.

But they'd had money in the past. He chewed his roll and considered that. He'd been so poor growing up that everyone looked rich to him. But the McCuens weren't poor by anyone's standards.

They'd kept their house maintained, at least back then. They'd owned good cars, and even taken vacations.

So where had the money gone? For medical bills after the accident? Or had the problems started sooner?

He was still thinking about that as he helped Erin dry the pans after dinner. The boys had already cleared the table, then crashed in front of the television with Grandma to watch the ball game.

"I've been wondering about something." He dried the roasting pan and set it on the counter. "Growing up, it always seemed like you had money. Aside from the house, I mean."

She rinsed the lid for the roaster under the faucet. "Well, I don't know how much money we had exactly. My grandparents never discussed that with me. But we certainly weren't broke."

"What about when your grandfather died? Is that when the problems started?"

"I don't think so. Grandma didn't act worried. In fact, she offered to pay my college tuition, but I had scholarships to cover the cost." She handed him the rinsed lid.

He dried it and put it on the roaster. "So your problems started after the accident. You used the savings to pay the bills."

She frowned. "There wasn't any money left to pay them. Grandma's account was already low."

"So you're saying she had money when your grandfather died, but it was gone by the time of the accident."

"I guess."

"So she must have spent it."

Her forehead creased. "I don't know. What would she have spent it on? She obviously didn't repair the house."

"Shopping sprees? A secret vice, like a gambling addiction?"

Erin grimaced. "Hardly. Besides, I would have noticed anything that odd. I lived at home, remember?"

"But the money was gone by the time she had the accident. And she'd developed this obsession by then."

Her gaze met his. "What are you saying? You don't seriously think the bank stole her money?"

"Do you?"

"Of course not. You know the Kells aren't thieves."

"Then why would she suspect them?"

"Senility. A lot of elderly people get that way." She drained the rinse water into a watering can and sponged down the sink. "You remember Mr. Blank?"

"The guy who ran the grocery store?"

She nodded. "He was convinced the government

was monitoring his phone calls. And Lottie's cousin thought the neighbors in her apartment building were spying on her through the vents."

"All right, so probably no one stole the money. But your grandmother believed they were trying to, and that's what counts." He draped the dish towel over his shoulder, leaned back against the counter and crossed his arms. "So what would you do if you thought the bank was embezzling your money?"

"Take the evidence to the police."

"And if there was no evidence?"

"I guess I'd take out whatever I had left to keep it safe."

"Do you think she did that?"

She shook her head. "I told you, there wasn't much to take out."

"How far do your records go back?"

"About three years."

"You don't have anything older than that?"

"Why?" Her eyes stayed on his. "You think she withdrew money after Grandpa died?"

"It's worth finding out."

Looking thoughtful now, she pulled the towel from his shoulder and wiped her hands, then hung it on the cabinet door. "I guess I could look through the boxes upstairs. When I moved Grandma into the study, I packed up all her papers to make more room. I intended to sort through them later, but I never had time."

She wrinkled her nose. "But if she did withdraw her money, where did she put it?"

"That's what we need to find out."

Chapter Thirteen

"I found them!" Erin gaped across the table at Wade. "I can't believe it. I actually found more bank statements. Look. They were stuck inside this magazine."

"Anything interesting in them?"

"I don't know yet." She set down the folder and opened it. Wade came around the table and leaned over her shoulder to see. Her skin prickled with awareness and she inhaled sharply. He had the most amazing effect on her. All he did was stand beside her and everything melted inside.

Forcing herself to concentrate, she checked the date on the statement. "Okay. We're looking at January, four years ago."

She skimmed down the withdrawal column and her breath caught. "Look. She took out five thousand dollars that month." She flipped to the next page and scanned it. "She did the same thing in February…and March."

Her hands trembling, she thumbed through the remaining statements, then lifted her stunned gaze to his. "And every other month that year."

He picked up the statements and leafed through them. "So in one year she withdrew sixty thousand dollars?"

Sixty thousand dollars. Her heart squeezed and she sucked at air.

"Is this all you've found?"

"So far."

He frowned. "The bank should have records going back further. You can get a copy from them."

"True." A smile tugged at her mouth. "But they're closed until Monday and I can't wait that long." She eyed the boxes on the floor beside her. "I've already looked through these, but there are three more boxes upstairs."

Her mind whirling, she rose from the table and closed the flaps on the boxes. Her grandmother had withdrawn sixty thousand dollars that year. But what on earth had she done with it?

And what if she found it? She quickly squashed that hope. Finding that money was like winning the lottery or Wade staying—extremely unlikely to happen. She'd just better hope that bank loan came through. Still…

She stood as Wade effortlessly lifted the boxes. Her gaze roamed his massive biceps and her pulse began to hum.

No matter how bad her finances were, her sex life was certainly great. She shivered as memories of the past night sizzled through her. The way his hard muscles bunched in her palms. The rasp of his breath in her ear. The way he held her, caressed her, as if he never wanted to stop.

She placed her hand on her sprinting heart and dragged in air. Wade had definitely taken over her heart, all right. But not her life. Maybe she'd better remind him of that. He had a tendency to take charge and do whatever he wanted.

"You know," she said carefully. "Once I get that bank loan, I'm going to pay back the money Norm lent me."

He paused, then deliberately set the boxes on the table. His gaze narrowed on hers. "I told you, I don't want it. And you agreed."

"I agreed to let you help me fix the house. Forgetting the loan wasn't part of the bargain."

"It was as far as I'm concerned."

"But—"

"Forget it. I'm not letting you pay me back."

"Letting me?" She scoffed. "I'll pay you back if I want to."

"You think so?"

"Absolutely." He stepped close, invading her space, forcing her to look up to meet his hard gaze. She instantly realized her mistake. Issuing a declaration was like waving a red flag at Wade. He liked nothing more than a challenge.

But despite her blunder, she wasn't going to back down. She had to show him she could cope.

She didn't move, and for a long moment, he just gazed at her. "Stubborn," he finally muttered. "Must be all that red hair."

She raised a brow. "It looks brown from where I'm standing."

"Oh, yeah?" A wicked glint lit his eyes. He traced a soft, slow path down her cheek with his finger, sending shivers over her skin. Then he cradled her jaw in his warm hand and urged her even closer.

His gaze caressed her face, her lips, and her breath backed up in her throat. Then he gently pressed his mouth to hers. His tongue blazed a path along her lips, teasing her with his heat.

Her heart zigzagged inside her chest. Pleasure shimmered through her nerves.

He lifted his head and she shuddered for more. "Wade…"

He smoothed her throbbing lips with his thumb, his face still inches from hers. His dark gaze hypnotized hers. Then he made a low sound and lowered his head.

His mouth fused with hers, more forcefully this time, and she shuddered with expectation. She opened to him, welcoming his tongue, his strength, wanting more than a simple kiss.

More than this moment. She urged him closer, deeper, with a yearning bordering on desperation.

But after a moment, he pulled away. His breathing rasped rough in her ear. "Forget the loan," he murmured.

His low voice mesmerized her, sending shivers along her skin and tempting her to obey. But no matter how much she needed this man, she couldn't let him run her life. "No."

He stilled and annoyance flared in his eyes. For several wild heartbeats, his hot gaze held hers.

Then the oven timer pinged. Her heart still thundering, she stepped back. She nearly ran to the counter in relief, grabbed the hot pads and checked the cake she'd made for the bake sale. Batter still clung to the toothpick, so she reset the timer and put the cake back in. That done, she dragged in her breath and turned back.

"This isn't settled," he warned.

It was for her. She opened her mouth to say so, then closed it again. After that kiss, maybe a strategic retreat would work best. When she didn't answer, he shot her a scowl, picked up the boxes and strode to the hall.

Her heartbeat still erratic, she returned to the table and sank into her chair. So he thought he'd make her forget the loan. But no matter how persuasive he was, she intended to solve her own problems.

Determined to concentrate on that task, she examined the statements again.

He returned a few minutes later with three more boxes. "This is the last of them."

"Thanks." Afraid that he would distract her, she avoided meeting his gaze. She waited until he started working on Norm's taxes again, then knelt and opened a box.

Just as the previous boxes had, this one contained newspaper articles about birds and roses, quilting magazines with the pages tagged, a few stray quilting blocks. Nothing that pertained to the bank.

She loaded the contents back into the box, closed the flaps and pushed it aside. There were even more magazines in the second box, but at the bottom she discovered a stack of manila folders. "I found something."

Her nerves drumming, she set the folders on the table and dropped into her chair. Wade came around and sat close beside her, his jeans-clad thigh touching hers.

She opened the top folder. "Okay. This looks like the year before the last set. So we're going backward by year."

Her excitement growing, she scanned the first statement. Then her breath hitched. "Look, another big withdrawal." Hardly breathing, she flipped the page. "And another. And another…"

Stunned, she lifted her gaze to his. "I can't believe this. She did it again. Five thousand dollars a month."

He grabbed the next folder and riffled through. "Here, too," he finally said, looking up. "Five thousand bucks, the first of every month."

They each opened another folder, but only found ordinary withdrawals. They finished the rest of the folders in silence, then Wade leaned back in his chair. "All right, so it looks like for three years, she seriously withdrew money, the same amount every month. Then she stopped."

"That's nearly two hundred thousand dollars." Erin's head felt light. That would have paid the medical bills, a new roof, Lottie's salary… "But what did she do with it?"

"You haven't found any clues?"

"No, but I still have one box to go through."

But the last box only contained more magazines. No receipts, no bills. No record of how she'd spent the money.

Deflated now, she dropped back into her chair and

propped her chin in her hands. She didn't know why she suddenly felt bleak. Nothing had really changed. But if her grandmother hadn't spent that money…

Wade leafed through the statements again, his brows lowered in concentration. "She sure ran through a lot of money."

"But what could she have spent it on?"

"You don't remember any expenses?"

At a loss, she shook her head. "She bought groceries every week, and fabric to add to her quilting stash. She was always making more blocks. A few clothes now and then, but she usually bought those on sale. And look." She picked up one of the statements. "She wrote checks every month and got cash from the ATM. That's how she paid her bills. So the five thousand dollars must have gone to something special."

"Maybe she gave it away, like to a charity."

"Then why didn't she just write a check?"

His forehead furrowed. "She might have been scammed. Maybe pressured to make bogus investments. A lot of old people get bilked out of their savings that way."

"I know." Dread tugged at her throat. "But she always seemed so sharp." Except for her obsession with the bank, but that had seemed harmless enough.

Guilt flooded through her. Why hadn't she watched Grandma better? "I should have paid more attention."

Wade reached over and picked up her hand. His rough fingers slid over hers. "It's not your fault," he said gently. "You couldn't control what she did."

"I should have tried." But she hadn't. And as a result, she'd failed on every front. She'd let her grandmother squander her money. She'd lost her job. And soon, she'd be the first McCuen in ten generations who couldn't hold on to the house.

Wade's warm hand squeezed hers and, despite her worries, she managed a smile. No matter what went wrong in her life, she could always depend on Wade.

"Any chance she'd remember what she did with it?" he asked.

"I doubt it. I can ask, but she only remembers bits and pieces of the past, like when Grandpa was alive."

The oven timer beeped. Wade released her hand and she rose and took out the cake. She turned it onto the cooling rack and glanced at the kitchen clock. "It's time for her nap now. I'll ask her once I get her settled." Although she doubted it would do any good.

But once Grandma was in bed, Erin hesitated to mention the bank and upset her. Stalling for time, she pulled the quilt over Grandma's shoulders and tucked it in. "I've always liked this quilt."

"It's a Dresden Plate."

"I know." Years back, Grandma had taught her the names of all the patterns and the story behind every quilt. She'd made this one soon after she'd married Grandpa. She'd cut the patterns out of feed sacks and appliquéd them to the background.

Erin's gaze lingered on the colorful flowers and dots, then dropped to the Prairie Point border. Of course, the quilting itself was exquisite. She ran her finger along the tiny stitches. Grandma had been so talented.

"I used to love it when Mrs. Neilands came by and

you sat in the sunroom to quilt," she said. "I'd organize your threads and make patterns with the pins in your pin cushions."

She gazed at Grandma's green eyes, so much like her own, and a thick lump formed in her throat. "Grandma, I hope you know how much I appreciate your letting me live here."

Grandma smiled, her eyes lost in the past. "We were so happy when you came. Such a joy."

"I've always loved it here. I just wasn't cut out to travel."

She'd hated traipsing around the globe with her jet-setting mother, staying with strangers, never belonging. Always a guest and imposition. And just when she'd start to feel settled, they'd fly to a new location.

"Dear Sandra," Grandma mused. "Like a butterfly. She just wanted excitement."

And Erin had wanted a home. Stability. A place where she wasn't cast off.

Where someone loved her.

"I'm just glad she left me here. And that you let me stay." For the longest time, she'd been terrified that she'd have to leave, that her mother would drag her back to that chaotic world, or that her grandparents wouldn't want her.

"Such a nice, little girl," Grandma sighed. "So quiet and helpful. So good."

And Wade had been so bad. Climbing high trees. Driving too fast. His daring and nerve had enthralled her.

Her face warmed. He was still a wicked man, but in a far more interesting way.

Grandma reached out and touched her hand. "...always wanted you to have this house. You belong here."

But she didn't have the money to keep it. Unless Grandma helped her. Her stomach tightened. "Grandma, I found some old bank statements today, and I noticed that a while back, you withdrew a lot of money."

Grandma's hand trembled on hers. "Thieves. They think I don't know."

Erin held her hand to calm her. "But why did you take out the money?"

"Stealing it. Have to be careful." She gripped her hand, her expression fierce. "The bank... Did you go?"

"Today's Sunday," she said patiently. "The bank's closed. But I'll check again tomorrow."

But what did she think was the point? The account was empty and had been for years. "Did you spend the money on something? Or maybe hide it so they wouldn't find it?"

A sly smile curved Grandma's lips. "They won't find it there."

Her heart stalled. Did Grandma remember? "Where?"

"Raincoat. In the closet."

Erin blinked. "You put money in your raincoat?" Oh, Lord. Stunned, she rose and rushed to the closet. She yanked apart the jammed hangars, pawing through until she spotted the trench coat, then carted it to the bed.

Hardly breathing, she watched Grandma fumble through one pocket, then the other. Then she pulled out a thick roll of bills. "Count it," she whispered.

Her nerves tensed, her hands shaking, Erin took the

money and unrolled it. Her heart slowed when she saw all the ones. She counted it out. Eighty dollars.

Her throat swelled with disappointment. "You were hiding this from the bank?"

"Stealing my money. They think I don't know."

"But, Grandma, you took out a lot more than this. What did you do with the rest?"

Grandma's eyes turned blank. "I…I…"

"Did you give it to someone? Did somebody need your help?"

"The bank… Stealing my money…"

"I know." A huge lump wedged in her throat. Grandma wasn't going to remember. She'd hoped, Lord, how she'd hoped, but it hadn't done any good.

Grandma thrashed against the pillow. "It's all right," Erin soothed. "Don't worry. Everything's going to be fine."

But was it really? She picked up Grandma's hand and stroked the soft, aged skin, caressing the knobby knuckles to calm her.

And fought off a wave of despair. Leaving Mills Ferry would devastate Grandma. She'd never survive the move.

But how could she keep her here? She couldn't continue like this much longer. She couldn't keep depending on Wade, or borrowing money to pay her bills.

Panic welled, but she tamped it down. Somehow she had to find a solution. And she had to do it fast.

Wade was leaning against the counter when she returned to the kitchen, his big hands braced behind him. "Did she remember anything?" he asked.

"Just this." She handed him the wad of bills, then slid into a seat at the table across from Sean. "She hid it in her raincoat so the bank wouldn't steal it."

Wade counted it, his dark brows lowered. "Eighty bucks? What happened to the rest?"

"Who knows? I'll go to the bank tomorrow, see if they remember anything. Maybe she told them what she planned."

"Not if she thought they were stealing it."

"It still won't hurt to check. I'll stop on my way to the airport." She paused. "Would you mind watching Grandma? Lottie comes in at ten."

"I can watch her," Sean said.

"You'll be in school." Wade pulled out the chair across from them and sat.

"I can miss it. We never do anything anyway."

"Right." The corner of her mouth quirked up. As if a teacher would buy that line.

"At least this tells us one thing," Wade said. "If she hid this money, she might have done the same with the rest."

She grimaced. "Yeah, and good luck finding it. It'll take forever to search this house."

Sean's eyes brightened. "You think there's a secret tunnel?"

"I doubt that, but the house was on the Underground Railroad." She thought for a moment. "That reminds me. There's a secret compartment in the parlor floor."

Sean straightened. "Really? Where? Can we open it?"

"Sure. It's under the braided rug."

Sean shoved back his chair and bolted into the parlor. Smiling, Erin followed more sedately with Wade. "You'll have to roll the rug up," she told him. "The compartment's right in the middle."

When Wade and Sean had rolled the rug back, she knelt on the floor and tested the boards. The loose one gave under her fingers. "Here it is. But I need something to pry it up."

Sean pulled a knife from his pocket. "Here."

She frowned at him. "You'd better not take that to school."

Sean and Wade knelt beside her as she slipped the knife under the edge of the board and pushed on the handle. The board popped up, and Wade moved it aside.

They all peered in. The hole was a foot deep and ran the width and length of the board. It was also empty.

"Damn," Sean said.

"Sean," Wade warned.

"Sorry."

Fighting her own disappointment, Erin handed the knife back to Sean. Finding that money would have certainly solved her problems.

"Interesting contraption." Wade examined the loose board, then set it over the hole.

"One of my ancestors hid paper and pencils there."

"That's lame," Sean said. "Why would they hide something dumb like that?"

"She was teaching her slaves how to read. That was illegal back then, so she hid the evidence under the floor."

"It was illegal? How come?"

"Maybe because if they knew too much, they'd rebel." She rose. "There are a lot of interesting stories about this house. I'll tell you some of them later."

"Are there ghosts?"

"Well, I've never seen one." She moved aside, and Wade unrolled the rug.

Then he braced his hands on his hips. "Any more hiding places?"

"In this house? Who knows?

"Besides the house, I mean."

"Well, the money wasn't in her car. It got totaled in the accident. And the mill is falling apart. I doubt she'd hide anything there."

"What kind of hobbies did she have?"

"Feeding birds, working in the garden, quilting."

"I'll check the shed," he said. "I noticed some old feeders and bags of birdseed. Flower pots, too. Maybe she stuck the money out there."

"Maybe she put it in a quilt," Sean said. "She told me how you stuff them with filling—"

"Batting." Erin smiled.

"Yeah. So she could have stuffed the money in there."

Wade looked doubtful. "That much money would be heavy. We're not talking about a few dollar bills."

"She could have divided it up," Sean persisted. "Maybe put it in more than one quilt."

"Maybe." Erin crinkled her nose. "But then she'd have to quilt through the money. But we can check," she said, noting his disappointment. "I don't want to rip the quilts apart, but we can feel them and see."

"She could have buried it," Wade said.

"I don't know. She wasn't that strong. But she did tend her roses a lot."

He shoved his hands into his pockets. "We'll check

the garden. We can get a metal detector and see if anything shows up."

"There might be one in the shed. My grandfather used a metal detector to hunt for Civil War bullets."

"Cool," Sean breathed. "Can I see if it's still there?"

"Sure."

Sean bolted from the parlor. A second later the front door slammed shut behind him.

Erin sighed. "He should wear a jacket. It's cold out there."

Wade slung his arm over her shoulder and walked with her to the foyer. The weight of his arm felt good. Secure. They stopped by the door and she turned into his arms.

"You don't really think we'll find the money, do you?" she asked.

"No." His gaze traveled over her lips, then back to her eyes. A grin tugged at his mouth. "But it'll keep Sean busy for a while. Maybe even give us a chance to be alone."

"More likely, we'll have every kid in Millstown out here searching for treasure."

He lifted her chin, and she looked into those whiskey-hued eyes. Absorbing his confidence, his strength. His concern.

"Don't worry about the money," he finally said. "We'll figure something out."

He lowered his head and slid his lips over hers. His kiss was warm and strong and solid, like Wade himself. Comforting, as she knew he meant it to be.

Then he broke the kiss, gave her neck a gentle squeeze and went out the door. She watched the door swing shut, then exhaled. He hadn't worn his jacket, either.

And he might not want her to worry, but she still had her debts to pay. She turned back toward the kitchen, pausing beside the ornate, claw-footed hutch.

Dread drummed through her stomach. She hated selling her inheritance, but what else could she do? How else could she generate income?

She scanned the beloved hutch, her throat thick, but knowing she didn't have a choice. Her gaze landed on a forgotten stack of mail and she reluctantly shuffled through it. More bills. Just what she needed. A sharp ache rapped through her skull.

But then she saw the bank's logo on an envelope and her hopes surged. She snatched up the letter and clutched it to her chest. Her loan came through. Thank goodness! Now she could pay some of those bills.

Smiling, she ripped open the envelope and scanned the letter. Then her breath stalled and her lips sank back into place. And suddenly, she felt sick.

The note was from Mike's father. He was sorry. He wanted to help her, but her credit was poor and he'd learned that she would soon be out of a job. He wished her the best of luck and very cordially, too.

But the loan had been denied.

Chapter Fourteen

Wade pulled Norm's pickup through the gates at Mills Ferry the next afternoon, swerved to avoid a pothole, then glanced in the mirror to make sure his load of boards hadn't shifted. Heaving a sigh, he mentally added another chore to his list. Unless he wanted his wheels knocked out of alignment, he had to level the driveway fast.

But when would he have the time? He needed to fix the turret, finish the roof…

A white panel truck parked by the porch caught his attention. As he approached, a short, stocky man walked to the driver's door and jumped in the cab. Wade swung wide to let the truck pass and caught the name on the side. Antietam Antiques. Erin must have sold more furniture.

Scowling, he parked behind her car and hopped out.

"Hey, Wade!" He looked up and saw Jay and Alex roaming the garden patch by the shed, holding metal detectors low to the ground. Sean trotted over, smiling broadly, a shovel slung over his shoulder. Excitement shone from his eyes.

"Look what we found. Civil War bullets!" He pulled a handful of lead balls from his pocket. "The guy from the antique store said they're real."

Wade picked up one of the ribbed bullets and brushed off the dirt, exposing the mottled lead. "Yeah. This is a Minie ball." He hefted it in his hand to check the weight. "Looks like you've got a good collection started." He set the ball back in Sean's palm. "What's Erin doing?"

"I don't know, but Lottie's looking through Grandma's clothes for money. We're checking the garden."

"Sounds like a plan." And his was to find out why Erin had sold more furniture. But he doubted he'd like the answer.

"How about taking a break and unloading these boards for me? You can stack them beside the sunroom."

"Okay."

His knee stiff, he limped up the front porch and entered the foyer. The hutch cabinet had disappeared. He scowled at the empty wall, then tramped down the hallway toward the kitchen. That woman had the damnedest pride. She'd sleep on the floor before she'd let him help her.

Voices came from Grandma's bedroom, so he detoured and stuck his head in the door. Lottie and

Grandma perched on the bed, surrounded by piles of clothes.

"Hi, Wade," Lottie said. "We're sorting out clothes for the rummage sale." She winked. "By the way, the realtor called while you were out. You got an offer on the house. She wants you to meet her at her office at six if you can. She sounded happy."

"Thanks." Someone must have offered the asking price on Norm's duplex. "I'll call her."

He strode from the bedroom into the kitchen. Erin stood at the table, examining a swatch of fabric. She looked up and the late afternoon sunlight heightened the circles under her eyes.

His scowl deepened. "Why did you sell the hutch cabinet?"

She frowned back. "Good afternoon to you, too."

He crossed his arms and she pulled her gaze away. She set the fabric on a pile and pulled another piece from the box beside her. After a moment she looked back up. "I didn't get the loan."

No surprise there. "So good old Mike didn't come through for you."

"Mike had nothing to do with it. He doesn't influence the bank's decisions. They turned it down because my credit's not good."

More likely because she'd lost her job—thanks to him. His mood darkened. "You found that out this morning?"

She pulled another quilt block from the box and studied it. "No, they sent me a letter in Saturday's mail."

But she hadn't told him then. So she was still secretive, still determined to solve her own problems. "So you sold your grandmother's hutch cabinet."

She coughed, set the fabric down on a different stack, and motioned toward the mail heaped on the counter. "The bills don't stop because I didn't get the loan."

"You don't have to sell your furniture. I'll pay the bills."

"It's my problem. I'll take care of it."

"For God's sake, Erin—"

"They're my bills and I'll pay them. I mean it, Wade."

He shoved his hands into his pockets, his frustration rising. Her pride was going to kill her. But what could he do about it? "So nobody at the bank knew what your grandmother did with the money?"

"No. Sue Barton remembered her withdrawing it, but it wasn't her place to ask. She assumed she was making some sort of payments."

"First time anyone in Millstown minded her own business."

"Unfortunately for us." She coughed again.

"What's wrong?" He eyed her pink nose. "Are you sick?"

"It's just a cold."

He kicked out a chair and sat. Her skin was pale, her eyes underscored with shadows. Worry and exhaustion lined her face. And she still refused to stop working.

And what little sleep she did get, he interrupted. Feeling guilty, he moved a pile of fabric aside and propped his elbows on the table. He either had to leave her alone or do more to solve her problems.

And he sure as hell couldn't keep his hands off her.

"Be careful you don't mix those squares up." She pulled a tissue from her pocket and blew her nose. "I'm saving that pile there." She nodded toward the taller stack. "The others go to the church rummage sale."

He looked at her in disbelief. On top of everything else, she was still volunteering. "No wonder you're sick. When was the last time you took a vacation?"

"The Caribbean cruise is next week." Shaking her head, she pulled out another quilt block.

He scowled back. If she wouldn't take care of herself, he would have to do it for her. "Let's drive up to Norm's cabin tonight."

"What?"

"His hunting cabin in the mountains in Pennsylvania. Nobody will bother us there. We can spend a few days, get some rest."

"I can't do that."

"Why not?"

Her mouth sagged. "I can't just drop everything and leave. I've got things to do. Commitments. The rummage sale's coming up, and I've got Sean and Grandma—"

"Lottie can handle them."

"And I have to work. The semester doesn't end until Christmas."

"You can call in sick."

"But I'm not sick. I've just got a cold."

He stared at her. "Isn't that the point of a substitute? So the teacher with the cold can stay home?"

She sighed. "I'm fine, Wade. And I want to work." She set the quilt block on the shorter pile.

Lottie stepped into the kitchen just then. "Erin, if you have a minute, Mae wants to talk to you."

"Sure. Any luck?"

Lottie held out a few crumpled bills. "Fifteen dollars stuck in a boot."

Erin sighed. "We'd better not throw away anything from now on unless we check it first. Who knows what she squirreled away."

"I'm sure she doesn't know. She was as surprised as I was when I pulled this out." Lottie handed the money to Erin. "I need to run down to the cottage to get a few things. Can you watch Mae until I get back?"

"Take your time. I'll sit with her until she falls asleep." She turned to Wade and frowned. "I'll be back in a bit."

He drummed his fingers on the table as she left, his frustration building. His gaze landed on the piles of fabric. He lifted a piece, frowned at the fancy stitches, and set it back down. He didn't know there could be so many fund-raisers in one town. And Erin volunteered at every one.

The telephone rang. Figuring the realtor was calling back, he rose and strode to the counter, pulled the phone off the hook and clicked it on. "Mills Ferry. Winslow here."

"Oh, hi, Wade. This is Julie. Brockman," she added, sounding miffed that he didn't recognize her voice. "Is Erin there?"

"Yeah, but she's busy with her grandma right now."

"Oh. Well, could you give her a message to call me? I wanted to see what time she can work the concession stand during the girls' basketball tournament. I need to firm up the schedule."

Another volunteer job. She had to be kidding. Erin was overworked enough.

And he was finally fed up. Someone had to force that woman to rest. "She can't do it."

"Can't do what?"

"The concession stand. She doesn't have time."

"What? But she always helps with the tournament. I can't believe—"

"Believe it. She's too busy."

A stunned silence followed that announcement. "I'll call back later," Julie finally said. "I'm sure she—"

He clicked off the phone. Didn't Erin have a life? The people in this town ran her ragged. She was broke and exhausted, and no one helped her back.

His gaze traveled to the stack of bills on the counter and his temper rose even higher. A business card lay next to the bills and he picked it up. Antietam Antiques. He tapped the card against his thigh and frowned. She would be ticked at his interference. Well, too damned bad. Somebody had to help her before she collapsed.

He looked at the card, then punched in the numbers on the phone.

"Antietam Antiques," a man answered.

Wade looked at the card. "Are you Bob Golden?"

"Sure am."

"Did you just buy a hutch cabinet from Erin Mc-Cuen?"

"That's right."

"I want to buy it back. And anything else you've ever bought from Mills Ferry."

A short silence ensued. "Well now, that's quite a list," Golden said.

"I figured that." He stuck the card in his back pocket. "Go ahead and start loading the truck. I'll stop by in a few minutes to pay for it. I'd like it delivered tonight."

He disconnected the line and looked at the pile of bills. If he was going to make her mad, he might as well aim for meltdown. He picked up her checkbook and voided the latest entries in the register. That done, he pulled the checks out of the unsealed envelopes, voided them, and ripped them up.

Then he scooped up the bills and headed up the stairs to grab his own checkbook.

An hour later Erin lugged the large garbage bag full of Grandma's old clothes into the hall and set it down. Then she turned back and quietly shut the bedroom door, careful not to wake Grandma. They hadn't discovered treasure in Grandma's room, but at least they could make a decent donation to the rummage sale.

Footsteps pounded up the porch, snagging her attention. Hoping to keep the noise down, she hurried into the foyer and swung open the door. One man stood on the porch holding a clipboard. Two others hoisted her hutch cabinet up the steps.

Perplexed, she glanced across the darkening yard to the white panel truck in the driveway. The tailgate was down and several pieces of furniture littered the grass.

"Ms. McCuen?"

"Yes?"

"Where do you want this hutch?"

Her gaze swiveled back to the man beside her. "I don't want it. I just sold it to Mr. Golden."

"Hold on," he told the men. They paused on the steps and he consulted his clipboard. "This is Mills Ferry, right?"

"Yes, but—"

"We're supposed to deliver this furniture here." He pulled a pink paper from his clipboard and handed it to her.

The paper had the Antietam Antiques logo scrawled across the top. She scanned the list of furniture. Her furniture. Everything she'd ever sold. But why would Bob send it back to her? Unless...

Her jaw tightened. *Wade.* She'd bet her house he'd done this.

"Ma'am?"

"Look." She held out a hand to stop them. "I need to straighten this out. Just, um, set that here on the porch for now. I'm going to find out what's going on. And don't unload anything else."

She marched down the hall to the kitchen, her annoyance mounting with every step. If he thought he could just take charge of her life...

She snatched the phone off the hook and tossed the furniture list on the counter. The counter where she'd left her bills. She stared at the pile of destroyed checks.

Furious now, she flipped open her checkbook and scanned the register. Then she snapped it shut. Darn that man! How dare he mess with her checkbook? He had some nerve paying her bills. And buying her furniture back! This was none of his business.

But what good would it do to call Bob Golden? If she returned the furniture, Wade would just buy it back again. He was that stubborn. The only solution was to pay Wade back and keep it.

She punched in the antique store's number. "Bob," she said when a man answered. "This is Erin McCuen."

"Erin." The man sounded jovial. "Did everything arrive all right?"

"I think so. They're unloading it now." A dull ache slid through her skull. "But I need to find out how much Wade paid so I can reimburse him, and it's not on this invoice."

"Well, I gave him a special price seeing how he was buying so many pieces."

"How special?"

"Well now, you can't expect me to sell things at cost. After all, I run a business here."

"I realize that. Just give me a general idea, so I can sort this out with Wade."

Golden paused. "Normally I would have doubled what I paid you, but I just tacked on twenty percent."

She closed her eyes. Her head felt light. She could never pay Wade back. Never. And he knew it. "Thanks, Bob."

She clicked off the phone, feeling sick. Wade had boxed her in, all right. He'd forced her to accept his help. And what could she do about it now? Her gaze landed on the voided checks and her stomach wrenched even tighter.

"Ma'am?" the man called from the foyer.

"I'll be right there." She returned the phone to its cradle. She had to accept the furniture. She couldn't waste more of the workers' time.

But as soon as he got home, she was going to deal with Wade Winslow.

* * *

Her temper had simmered into full-blown anger by the time Wade strolled into the kitchen two hours later. She leaned back against the sink and crossed her arms.

Their gazes met and he paused. His eyes narrowed fractionally, then he turned and propped the hunting rifles he was carrying in the corner. He pulled a box of shells from his jacket pocket and set it on the table, then braced his hands on his hips.

His eyes met hers again. He looked calm, confident. Not the least bit repentant. And that made her even madder.

"You might as well let me have it," he finally said.

"Don't you dare trivialize this. Or me!" She marched across the kitchen to the table. "You had no business getting in my checkbook and paying my bills. No right at all. That was invasive. Rude! My checkbook and my bills are my private property."

"You're right. It was rude."

"And the furniture. I can't believe you bought that back."

"Believe it."

"At twenty percent more than he paid me?"

"He gave me a special price."

Her frustration rose. "Don't try to be cute. I'll never be able to pay you back. I don't have that kind of money and you know it."

His gaze darkened. "I don't want you to pay me back. It's a gift."

"A gift?" She scoffed. "A gift is a bouquet of flowers or a box of chocolates. You don't buy a truckload of antiques as a gift."

He lifted his wide shoulders. "I can afford it. I just sold Norm's house."

"That's not the point."

"So, what is the point? That I hurt your pride? Okay, I'm sorry. I was trying to help you. Look, if it makes you feel better, think of it as a favor."

"A favor?"

"Sure. I just did you one, so now you can pay me back. I'd like to store Norm's tools in your shed, and I need a place for his guns."

Her heart hitched. He wanted to store things here. Storing meant temporary. That he wasn't staying. The bottom of her stomach swooped.

She'd known he would leave. She'd expected it from the start. But not yet. Not now. And hearing it made it so much worse.

She whirled around and staggered back to the sink. A deep pain gripped her chest, an emptiness that threatened to swamp her. But she couldn't let Wade see it. She had too much pride for that.

Gathering her dignity, she turned to face him again. "Call it whatever you want, but it doesn't change anything. You're not waltzing in here and taking over my life, when you're only going to leave."

He stilled. "You knew I wouldn't stay."

"And I never asked you to. That's not the point."

"Sure it is." He stood frozen, his eyes panicked.

"No, it's not." Her stomach wrenched. "I never expected you to stay." But she'd let herself hope. Dear

Lord, she had hoped. No matter how frantically she'd warned herself not to.

"Erin," he pleaded.

Her emotions raw, she lashed back. "You're just feeling guilty. You want to pay my debts so you can leave with a clear conscience."

Bingo. She saw the truth in his eyes.

Pain ripped her chest and she reeled back. He'd paid her bills to appease his conscience. Oh, God.

"Damn it," he said. "You've twisted this all around."

"Have I?" She felt flayed. "This isn't about helping me at all, is it? You're just making it easier for you to leave."

The telephone rang but she didn't move. Then it rang again. Her hands trembling, her heart crumbling, she walked over and jerked up the receiver. "Hello?"

"Hi, Erin? This is Julie."

"Oh, hi, Julie." She kept her eyes on Wade as he stalked across the kitchen toward her.

"Listen, I think there's been a misunderstanding. I called earlier and Wade said you weren't going to work the concession stand at the basketball tournament this year."

"What?"

"He said you were too busy. I knew there had to be a mistake—"

He grabbed the phone from her hand. "She'll call you back," he told Julie, then clicked it off and set it on the counter.

She snatched the phone back up. "Of all the… How dare you tell her what I'll do?"

"You're working too hard. You need to rest."

"I can decide that for myself."

"Yeah? Well, so far your decisions have made you sick. If you don't have the sense to take care of yourself, then someone else has to do it."

"You think I don't have sense?" she sputtered. "Just because I caught a cold? One little cold gives you the right to direct my life?"

He crossed his arms. "You can't turn her down, can you?"

"What?"

"If you can decide, then go ahead and decide not to do it. Call her back and tell her you're too busy."

"But I'm not too busy."

"Sure you are. Unless you're too sick, you're going out with me that night."

"But I want to help—"

"I dare you." His hard gaze bore into hers. "Call her back and tell her you're busy. Three words, Erin. Three lousy words. *Sorry, I'm busy.* Go ahead. Call her back and tell her."

She hesitated. Her grip tightened on the phone.

"Do it."

Her hands trembled. Her pulse surged loud in her ears. She wanted to prove him wrong. She wanted to wipe that smirk off his face. But he was right. She couldn't make the call.

"Say it, Erin. *Sorry, I'm busy.*"

She fought back a swell of nausea.

"Afraid they won't like you if you turn them down?" His voice was soft, flat. His gaze stayed hard on hers.

He was right. Dear Lord, but he was right. She was still that little girl begging for acceptance. Trying to please everyone, to make them need her, so they wouldn't make her go.

So they'd love her. Unlike her mother.

She clamped a hand over her mouth. She felt sick. Weak. Her hand shook so hard she could hardly punch in the numbers.

"Hello?" Julie answered.

She opened her mouth. The words jammed in her throat.

"Hello?"

"Julie, I…" She jerked in a breath. "I'm sorry. I— can't help out this year. I…I'm busy."

Wade took the receiver from her hand and disconnected the line. He set the phone on the counter and reached for her, but she wrenched herself away. Nausea roiled through her stomach so strong that she thought she might faint.

"Erin."

"Leave me alone." Her eyes burning, she lurched back to the table. She blindly grabbed quilt blocks and stuffed them into the box. She felt raw, exposed. Flayed by the truth she now had to face.

"Erin," he said again, from close behind her. His voice was sympathetic.

But she didn't want his sympathy, his pity. She didn't want his help or his guilt. Her vision blurred. Her chest cramped. She shoved the rest of the blocks in the box.

"God, Erin. I'm sorry." He wrapped his arms around her from behind.

"Don't touch me. Please. I want to be alone." She picked up the box and jerked away.

He reached for her again and she stumbled back. The box fell, spilling quilt blocks onto the floor.

She knelt to pick them up and wiped back the hot stream of tears. Lord, she was pathetic. Pleading for acceptance all these years. For love.

Just as she had with Wade. Hoping that if she were nice enough, if she cared enough, he'd love her back. But he didn't. He was still going to leave.

She felt him stoop down beside her, but she refused to meet his eyes. She couldn't take his compassion right now. She felt too vulnerable, too exposed. She shoved fabric back into the box.

Desperate to get away, she scooped up an armful of quilt blocks. She coughed and lost her grip. The fabric slid over her knees.

"Erin." His voice sounded distant. Strangled.

She blinked through the blur of tears, then leaned forward to gather it up again.

"Erin," he said again, sounding urgent.

She sniffed and wiped her eyes with her sleeve.

"I'll be damned," he said.

She paused, then blinked at the papers lying amid the quilt blocks. The strange sight penetrated her misery and she blinked again. "Are those…?"

"Savings bonds." Dozens of them. He picked one up. His incredulous gaze met hers. "Ten thousand bucks a piece."

Chapter Fifteen

Still reeling from their discovery, Erin placed the last stack of savings bonds on the table, then slid into a seat across from Wade. Astounded, she stared at the piles in front of her. She couldn't believe they'd found all these bonds.

She picked up one of the taller stacks and shuffled through it. "Well, this accounts for the money Grandma took out."

"I'll say."

Still overwhelmed, she shook her head. "This is just so amazing. I wonder what made her buy all those bonds?"

"Whatever the reason, she'd been at it for a while." Wade nodded toward the older, Series E bonds they'd set to the side. "She bought the double Es just before the accident, but those thousand-dollar bonds go back decades."

Erin picked up a pile of bonds and flipped through it. The oldest ones dated back to the forties, when her grandparents married. "I'll bet Grandpa bought these."

"Why do you say that?"

"Because it fits. He never trusted banks. He grew up during the Depression, and was always talking about how tough life was then, like how they made sandwiches out of butter and onions. Or how they got weighed at school to see if they were too thin. He hated that because they made him take off his shoes, and he had big holes in his socks."

"He was lucky to have shoes. I'm sure my grandparents didn't."

"I know. But everyone had to scrabble for money."

He leaned back in his chair. "So when he did have money, he wanted to keep it safe. And government bonds were about as safe as you could get."

Her heart swelled. Dear Grandpa, putting away his hard earned money all those years. Buying savings bonds to make certain it stayed safe. And he'd succeeded. Now she could use that money to save Mills Ferry.

"But then what made your grandmother buy them?"

"Maybe once she got it in her head that the bank was stealing her money, she remembered that Grandpa bought bonds. And if he thought they were safe…"

Suddenly it all seemed clear. Why hadn't she thought of bonds sooner? She should have figured it out, even if her grandmother had forgotten.

"We can check at the bank to see how much they're worth," Wade said. "The oldest ones have matured, but they keep earning interest for a while, so they're probably worth more than their face value. The recent ones could be less. But even so, you've got a good chunk of money."

Enough to pay off her loans, her credit card debts, the medical bills… Enough to repair the house and pay back Wade. Enough to solve all her problems.

Except for one. Wade's whiskey-colored eyes met hers. Her stomach dropped and a terrible, sinking sensation swept through her.

"Erin—"

"I don't want to talk about it."

"We have to deal with it sometime."

"But not now. Not tonight. Please?" Dread lurched through her heart. She couldn't bear to think about it, let alone voice what they both knew.

That now, with her financial problems solved, there was no reason left for him to stay.

Later that night, Erin stood at the bedroom window. The wind had come up, thrashing branches against the moonlit sky. She felt depleted. Drained. And she still couldn't believe her troubles were over.

Wade moved behind her, wrapped his strong arms around her waist and rested his cheek against hers. Her heart full, she leaned back against him, absorbing his strength and warmth. Life certainly took some strange turns. Miracles happened, like finding those bonds. Or Wade coming back to her—at least for a time.

He slid his hands under her sweater and his warm, calloused palms caressed her belly. She shivered. How she loved this man. She closed her eyes, relishing his sensuous, masculine scent, the feel of his bristled cheek against hers. The wonder of having him with her tonight.

He nuzzled her neck with his mouth, and sparks ran over her body. With a sigh, she reached back and stroked the hairs at his nape, felt the sinew beneath his hot skin.

More insistent now, he moved his hands to her breasts and pushed up her bra. His rough fingers slid over her sensitive skin, jolting her with pleasure. Her nipples beaded hard in his palms.

She couldn't resist him. One touch, and he heated her body. One touch, and she shattered with need. She hungered for this man, body and soul.

He moved closer. She felt his arousal against her buttocks, his hot kisses along her neck. Heat pulsed through her, spiraling to an urgent ache.

Growing impatient, she turned her head and his lips moved over hers. She parted her lips, craving his tongue, his mouth, his body. Her heart clenched, then throbbed with insistent wanting.

She wanted to feel him, all of him. She wanted to stroke his neck, his shoulders, his jaw. To memorize every inch of him. His smell and his feel. The taste of his mouth and skin.

Because each kiss could be the last. Each touch could signal the end. Her stomach wrenched and she turned fully into his arms, fueled by desperation. She didn't want him to leave.

She broke away. "Wade, I…"

Despair threatened, and she squeezed her eyes against the onslaught of tears. No, she couldn't think about it. Not tonight. Please not tonight. She just wanted to spend this one last night together. To savor every second, every touch. So she could remember it when he was gone. And relive it in her dreams forever.

Dawn came too soon. The wind had increased overnight, making the trees moan in the early light. Their lovemaking had been urgent, desperate. Tender and poignant. They'd said through actions what neither dared to say out loud. *Goodbye.*

Erin had lain awake long afterward, her heart aching, and listened to him breathe. Making herself accept that he would go.

She slid out of the warm bed and donned her robe against the chill. Then she crossed to the window and looked out. Branches swayed in the wind and she shivered. All night long, she'd searched for a solution. She hadn't found one.

She couldn't ask him to stay. She loved him far too much to trap him. He had to decide to stay for himself.

Because he'd been absolutely right yesterday. She'd spent her entire life trying to make people need her, and she refused to do that with Wade. She wouldn't, couldn't, chain him to her. She had to let him be free— even if it meant he left her.

"We need to talk," he said from the bed.

She stiffened. Words of denial crowded her throat. She relentlessly beat them back. She couldn't put it off forever. "I know," she whispered.

He rose from the bed, pulled on his jeans and T-shirt, and joined her at the window.

She forced herself to meet his gaze. Her stomach balled into a knot.

His jaw was set, his eyes serious. "You knew I couldn't stay."

"Yes, I know." Her stomach plunged.

"It has nothing to do with you. You have to know that." He reached out and fingered a strand of her hair. "God, Erin. You're everything to me. Everything I could ever want.

"And you know I'd stay if I could. If things were different. If I were different. But I'm not right for you."

Her heart throbbed. Tears ravaged her throat. "Don't you think I should decide that?"

He shook his head, his eyes tortured. "You can't. There are parts of me you don't know. That you don't want to know."

Her heart twisted. "You're wrong. I know everything about you. I always have."

"No, you don't." He dropped his hand and scowled at the morning sky. "I'm not the man you think I am. I can't be. And God knows I've tried."

Her throat full, she gazed at him. He was so hard on himself. And so good. He always did the right thing, even if it meant he suffered.

He thought he had to leave for her sake. He was wrong. Dead wrong. Because she did know him. Completely.

And maybe it was time he found that out. Her heart rapping hard against her rib cage, she walked to the dresser and pulled open the bottom drawer. Then she lifted the quilt and took out the framed poem she'd hidden there when he first arrived.

For a minute she just gazed at the crinkled paper inside the glass. It was a time of truth, all right. A time to lay open the past and bare her soul.

And hopefully, a time for healing. She walked back and handed it over.

"What's this?" He took the frame from her hands and frowned down at it. She knew the moment he recognized it. His eyes widened and he went completely still. Then his gaze slowly rose to hers. He looked stunned. Exposed.

Then he averted his gaze to the window. His Adam's apple dipped. For several long seconds, he didn't speak.

"Where did you get it?" he finally asked, his voice subdued.

"The trash. As soon as class was over, I took it out."

He braced his arm on the glass and hung his head. Her heart ached watching him. Knowing how vulnerable he felt, how raw.

"How…" He cleared his throat. "How did you know I wrote it?"

"I saw it on your desk. I was so surprised that you'd done your homework." Tenth-grade composition, and they'd had to write a poem. But then the teacher announced that they would read them out loud. And Wade had slowly crumpled his up.

When his turn came, he claimed he didn't have it. The teacher promptly sent him to the office for not participating in the class. And as he sauntered out the door, the epitome of cocky rebellion, he'd tossed his wadded poem in the trash.

She'd retrieved it as soon as the bell rang. And then read the poem that laid bare his soul. Where he'd confessed his need for acceptance. His shame. His fear that he was empty inside. That he wasn't worth loving.

And in that moment, the crush she'd had on him all

those years had blossomed into love. Real, abiding love. Because she knew him down to his soul.

She sucked in her breath. She had to tell him. Her knees trembled and a queasy feeling seeped through her heart. She was terrified to say it, to put it into words. The risk to her heart was enormous. But his needs were greater than her fears. He needed to know the truth, for his sake.

"I love you," she said.

He froze. The words hung in the silence between them. Awkward. Unwelcome. Her heart plummeted at the truth in his eyes. He didn't love her back. Oh, God.

But she couldn't retract the words. And she didn't want to. The time for hiding had passed.

"I always have." She brazened on. "And you're wrong. I do know you. I know everything about you, even your fears. And I love you anyway."

He turned to face her. "Erin…" His expression was blank, his eyes distant. He was retreating, erecting his walls, closing her off.

Her throat closed up, and fierce pain knifed her heart. Oh, Lord. It hurt far worse than she'd expected. To finally risk it all, to confess her love, just to have him reject her.

"I don't expect you to love me back." Her voice wobbled, and she inhaled a tremulous breath. "And I don't expect you to stay. You never do. That's how you cope."

She managed a sad smile. "You see, we're the same, Wade. Two abandoned kids, thinking nobody wants us. You were right yesterday. I tried to make everyone need me. You just don't let anyone close. You leave before they can abandon you."

Tears welled and she blinked them back. "But no matter what, you need to know that somebody really does love you."

She took the poem from his hand, walked over to the bed and hung it in its place on the wall. Where it had hung for years. Where it would stay forever.

Then, her heart breaking, she turned and left the room.

Chapter Sixteen

The sharp crack of splintering wood broke the turret's silence. Wade repositioned the chisel and hammered down on the windowsill again. Pieces of decayed wood fractured and fell to the floor amid the sawdust.

The sill had rotted out, just like his life. He pried up a stubborn remnant of the shattered wood with his hammer and yanked it loose. He'd screwed up, all right. Big time. He should never have given in to his needs and slept with Erin.

Remorse soured his gut. He hated the pain he'd seen in her eyes, hated himself even more for putting it there. He'd never intended to hurt her.

But he couldn't give her what she wanted or needed. Marriage. Commitment. Panic knifed his gut at the thought.

He straightened and ran his hand down his face. So,

he would go. He had no reason to linger. He'd finished most of his executor duties and Erin didn't need his rent anymore. In fact, he should feel relieved. Happy. He'd wanted to leave Millstown and now he had his chance.

His gut tightened at that thought and anxiety hammered his nerves. But how could he leave Mills Ferry? How could he bear to lose Erin?

He sucked in his breath, feeling caged, trapped by the dread that had paralyzed him all day. He couldn't stay. He had no doubts about that. But damned if he could go.

He bent, picked up the board he'd cut to replace the old sill and tapped it into place. Footsteps thumped up the stairs and he grimaced. That was another problem. How could he leave the kids, especially Sean? Even if he hadn't made promises, he felt like a coward slinking off.

Frowning at the mess he'd made of his life, he fished a handful of brads from his tool belt and anchored the sill to the casing.

"Hey, Wade," Sean said. Wade glanced up as Sean crossed the turret, trailing footprints in the sawdust. Jay followed close behind him.

Wade paused, distracted by the seriousness of Sean's expression. "School get out early?"

"Yeah, the teachers had a meeting." Sean's gaze didn't quite meet his.

Wade looked at Jay, who quickly turned and peered out the window. His instincts stirred. Something was wrong, all right. He hooked his hammer in his tool belt and crossed his arms. "A meeting, huh?"

"Yeah."

"This meeting have anything to do with you?"

"No." Sean still looked away. "It was just some in-service thing."

"So what's the problem?"

"Nothing." Sean shuffled his shoe in the dust.

His gut tightened. "You see your father by any chance?"

"No way!"

He eased out his breath. Thank God for that. But then what was the problem? He slanted his head. "Jay?"

The older teen shrugged. His T-shirt was torn along the collar and grass stains climbed up the back.

"Looks like you had a fight," Wade said.

"Yeah."

"Care to tell me what about?"

"Nothing," Jay muttered. "Just some dumb kid smarting off."

Right. He drilled his gaze at Sean. "You might as well tell me the whole story. I'll hear it sooner or later."

"It was Erin."

"Erin?" He blinked, taken aback.

"Yeah. He called her a...you know... I mean, since you're living together and all."

Wade's stomach clenched. Of course rumors would be flying about them. Nothing stayed a secret in this town. Especially after that kiss.

A sick feeling seeped through his gut. He'd anticipated those rumors from the start. Hadn't he told everyone he was renting a room, to try to avoid this conclusion? So why hadn't he moved out after Norm died and salvaged her reputation?

Sean's voice dropped to a whisper. "He said she got

fired because you guys are…you know, shacking up, and that makes her a, you know…"

Wade stilled. So that kiss hadn't cost her her job. She'd lost it because he lived here.

His gut tightened. Why hadn't she told him the truth? He could have moved out and stayed at Norm's duplex. She shouldn't have sacrificed her job for him.

He speared his hand through his hair. He'd fouled up everything for that woman, done nothing but cause her more pain. And this was just one more reason to leave, although it was probably too late to do any good.

It might even affect Sean's custody issue if he'd damaged her reputation too badly. Dread drummed through his gut. Had he botched that, too?

Disgusted at the mess he'd created, he shifted his gaze to Jay. "Thanks for defending Erin."

"That's okay." Jay turned back, fingering his swollen lip.

"You need some ice?" Wade asked.

"Nah."

He nodded. "How's the other guy look?"

"Bad." Sean grinned. "Jay busted him up pretty good."

Wade smiled back. At least Erin would have some staunch defenders when he was gone. When he'd abandoned her and returned to Montana. His smile faded.

"Anything I can do?" Sean asked.

He reluctantly brought his attention back to his project. "Sure. As soon as I sink these nails, you can fill the holes with putty and caulk around the edges."

"What about me?" Jay asked.

"Want to remove the old sills?"

"Okay."

Still feeling disturbed, he made sure the new sill was secure, then picked up the backsaw and glanced around the turret. "We might as well work our way around the room so we can keep the tools together."

He limped to the next window and pulled it open. "Make sure you don't cut into the stool. That's this part here." He made several cuts with the backsaw to demonstrate, then loosened a piece of the sill with the chisel. "And check for nails. You might have to pry some sections up. I'll cut the new boards while you're doing that."

He stepped back and supervised for a moment. Then, satisfied that Jay knew what he was doing, he strode over to retrieve the caulking gun.

A puff of smoke caught his attention and he squinted out the window at the distant trees. Some fool was burning trash, despite the county-wide ban—and on a windy day, too.

He wondered who lived over there. Frowning, he picked up the caulking gun and loaded it. He didn't recall any houses along that stretch of the river, just Battle-Ax Bester's inside the canyon.

Still thinking that over, he walked over to Sean. "You ever caulk before?"

"No."

"Hold it at an angle." He put the gun at a forty-five degree angle to the edge. "And slant it a bit. You won't need too wide of a bead." He demonstrated, then handed the gun to Sean.

"Not so fast. There you go." He watched Sean inexpertly apply the caulk. He'd get the hang of it. The kid learned fast.

Figuring he'd better measure each sill individually before he cut the boards, he pulled the tape measure from his tool belt. Nothing in a house this old came in a standard size.

He walked back toward Jay and his gaze rose to the far window again. Coils of black smoke now rose from the woods and mushroomed into heavy billows. His eyes narrowed. That didn't look like a trash fire anymore. The wind gusted and red flames licked the trees. "Oh, hell."

"What's wrong?"

"The woods are on fire." His pulse rising, he strode across the room to the window, using the advantage of the turret's height to survey the area. Luckily the fire wasn't big yet, less than a dozen acres, but the wind was spreading it fast.

He thought hard. The river would contain the south side, but to the west lay the open canyon where Mrs. Bester lived. Worse yet, the gusts could spread the north flank toward town.

An intense calm settled over him as he slipped into his fire boss role. The county road dropped in from the rim of the canyon, but going in that way would put him at the head of the fire. He'd do better driving up the towpath that fronted the river.

Another flame whipped upward and his adrenaline surged. The fire was moving quickly. "I've got to stop that before it reaches town."

"We'll help," Sean said.

"Forget it. You're staying here." He untied his tool belt and dropped it to the floor.

"Why? We can help," Sean protested.

"Too dangerous." The wind could shift; they could get hit by a falling snag… He shook his head.

"But that's what hotshots do," Jay said.

"Yeah, but they're professionals. They've been trained."

"So you can train us. Besides, you can't stop a fire by yourself."

That was true. One person couldn't beat a fully engaged fire in this wind. And by the time the fire department called in their volunteers, half the town could be gone.

"All right," Wade said, reluctantly. "As long as you do exactly what I say. And I mean *exactly*. And as soon as the fire department arrives, you're out of there."

"All right!" Both boys grinned.

He blew out his breath, hoping he wouldn't regret this. "Come on. We need to catch that fire." He turned and sprinted to the door, then lumbered down the stairs. The kids thundered close behind him.

Erin was standing in the foyer when they ran past. "Call 9-1-1," he called. "There's a fire upriver toward the canyon. We'll try to hold it until they get there."

Alex and another teen were coming up the driveway when he rounded the porch. "Get in the truck," he shouted.

He ran into the shed and pulled out the tools he had on hand—a pickax and shovels, Norm's chain saw, an extra can of fuel—and handed them to Sean. He didn't have a water pump, but he'd just have to make do.

The kids piled into the back of the truck with the tools. He leaped into the cab and gunned the engine, then careened down the trail to the river. By the time they'd lurched up the towpath to the fire, bright orange flames lit the sky.

His adrenaline surged. The drought had dried the woods into tinder and the wind gusts would spread the flames fast, especially with the dried leaves littering the ground. Luckily, the temperature was down. That was the only thing in their favor.

He hopped from the truck and immediately coughed. Smoke hovered over the towpath and ashes dusted his shoulders. Flames shot through the parched trees.

He quickly pulled the tools from the truck. "Here's what we're going to do." He shouted to be heard above the roar of the fire. "We're going to dig a fire line, a trench, up the north flank so the fire doesn't move toward town. I'll use the chain saw to cut back trees. Jay, you follow me with the pickax and scratch out the trench. It needs to be pretty wide. Sean and Alex can shovel behind you and throw the dirt on the flames."

"What should I do?" the new kid yelled.

Wishing again that they had a pump, he glanced around. A spruce tree stood nearby, so he jogged over and sawed off a bough. He dragged it back to the kid. "Use this to beat back any spot fires that pop up. We don't want them slopping over our line."

The kids smiled in obvious excitement. He grinned back, knowing exactly how they felt. He experienced that same exhilaration, that thrill of the challenge, every time he battled a blaze. "Okay, hotshots. Let's show Millstown how to catch a fire!"

Carrying the chain saw and fuel can, he loped through the woods toward the flames. When he reached the tail of the fire, he cranked up the saw and started on the first tree. The kids immediately set to work behind him.

Sawdust spewed from the tree as he expertly angled his saw. He held steady, inhaling smoke and pine, until the tree toppled in toward the fire. Satisfaction surged through him. One down. He stepped over to the next tree.

His saw buzzing, his adrenaline rushing, he focused on the job. They were going to have a tough time fighting this fire, especially if the wind picked up. There weren't any roads or other firebreaks to keep it from spreading. Even if the fire department got here and pumped water up from the river, they still needed to build a strong line.

The next tree fell and he glanced back to check on the boys. Jay, the strongest of the bunch, swung the pickax and scratched out the fire line. Behind him, Sean and Alex widened the trench and shoveled dirt on the flames. Even the new kid jumped around with his spruce branch and beat back sparks in the grass.

His chest swelled. The kids hadn't hung back, hadn't balked, even with hot ashes falling around them. They were a courageous bunch.

Confident they could manage, he turned his attention back to the fire. It wasn't huge yet, maybe a couple dozen acres, but the wind was throwing up embers and torching spot fires yards away. And with every passing moment, the front grew more erratic.

Concentrating now, he continued sawing his way up the flank. The wail of the chain saw suspended his sense of time. He worked steadily, tree after tree, man against nature, just dripping sweat and cutting wood. Sucking up dust and sawing down trees. Doing what he knew, what he loved.

And the kids kept with him, never complaining, never slowing their pace. Even when he finally paused to refuel the chain saw, they didn't stop working. He felt a fierce rush of pride. He'd never seen a better crew.

He eyed the fingers of fire creeping ahead of their line, the smoldering stumps glowing bright amid the black trees. Suddenly a hiss from behind caught his attention.

"Alex, look behind you," he yelled.

"Got it." Alex darted over and stomped out the flare-up.

"Keep checking back in case sparks blow over the line," he told the new kid.

"Okay." The boy immediately headed back to patrol the trench.

Reassured that the kids could handle their jobs, Wade focused on advancing the line. Yard by yard they moved relentlessly toward the canyon, choking down smoke laced with pine tar and securing the flank. The wind sporadically fanned flames in their direction, but they still defended their ground.

When they finally reached a small rise, he cut off the chain saw. "Hold up," he shouted. "Let's take a break." The kids immediately trotted over. They were panting, sweating, their faces streaked with grime. And they were grinning like crazy.

He smiled back. "You've done a good job," he said. "You held this flank and saved Millstown."

His chest tightened and he felt a strong surge of satisfaction. Just like he felt with his smokejumping bros. Maybe more.

The realization surprised him, but it was true. He liked leading the kids and being a role model. The job suited him. And, even more surprisingly, he didn't want to give it up.

"Winslow!" someone shouted over the snapping fire. He turned and saw his former classmate, Butch Ableson, jog toward him with a radio in his hand.

"What's going on?"

Butch stopped and gasped for breath. "We got two pumps on the towpath, but we can't move any closer. We called Pennsylvania and West Virginia for help, but everyone's on a fire in Berkeley County. It's going to take them a while to get here."

Sparks scattered their way. Wade frowned. "The front's moving toward that canyon. The way this wind is gusting, it could blow up at any time." And the fire would barrel right through with nothing to stop it. "Is everyone out of there?"

"We're not sure. We got Bester on the phone and told her to get out, but we don't know if she made it. She stopped answering her phone and nobody's seen her car."

Wade swore. Her house sat just inside the canyon. If she didn't leave soon, she'd be trapped.

"I'll send someone around on the county road," Butch said.

"You can't get in there. If the fire blows up, that road will be engulfed."

Just then, the flames surged forward and his stomach tensed. They were running out of time. If Bester was in there, they had to get her out now.

Butch's radio crackled. "I've got to get back," he yelled a minute later. "There's a problem with the pumps."

"I'll get Bester," Wade promised. But how? He eyed the road running uphill out of the canyon. They'd never outrun the fire. Dread prickled over his skin. The place had entrapment written all over it.

Getting to her wasn't a problem. He had a direct path in there from where he stood. But with the fire burning behind him, he couldn't use the same way out. There was no escape route, and he didn't have time to make one.

Raw fear slinked down his spine and for the first time ever, he balked at doing his job. He didn't want to risk it, and he sure as hell didn't want to die—not when he finally had something to live for.

His breath stalled and his head felt light. It was true. He did have something to live for. The kids. *Erin.* His heart jerked, then swelled with longing.

And love. He loved her. He always had.

He stared at the billowing smoke and finally acknowledged the truth. The reality he'd evaded for years. He loved Erin.

And he could trust her. She'd stood up for him, defended him her entire life. Hell, she'd even sacrificed her job for him, at the risk of losing Mills Ferry. And she would never abandon him—because she loved him, too.

A huge peace filled his soul. He didn't have to run anymore. Everything he needed was here in Millstown—with Erin, where his heart had been all along.

The fire pulsed. Sparks showered down on them again and they all jumped back. The kids stomped down the tiny flares.

A stark feeling wrenched his gut, along with a sense of doom. No matter how reluctant he was to do it, he had to go in there to rescue Bester. He didn't have a choice.

Even if he didn't come out alive.

"All right, guys," he said. "Listen up. I'm going in to get Mrs. Bester. I want you to burn off that strip of grass." He pointed to a narrow area leading along the edge of the canyon. The dry grass would burn out quickly—unless the main fire blew up and engulfed it first.

Sean's jaw slackened. "You want us to spread the fire?"

"I need you to make an escape route so I can get back out. Once that fuel burns off, the main fire will go around it." He glanced around. "Who's got lighters?"

Jay and Alex each pulled one out. "Light some dry branches and spread it fast," he instructed. "Once you get it going, get the hell out. That way." He pointed back along the flank toward the river. "Don't wait for me. Do you understand?" He couldn't risk the fire shifting and catching the kids.

They nodded. Their eyes looked huge, their expressions scared. "You did a great job today." He looked at each of their faces and his chest squeezed tight. "I'm damn proud of every one of you. Now get to work."

He turned, crashed through a patch of low brush, then angled down toward the house. He slowed just enough to glance back at the kids. They were busy lighting the grass. Sean lifted his hand in farewell.

His throat cramped and the bitter irony struck him. After all these years, he'd finally found the woman who loved him, and the place where he belonged. He'd found heaven. And now he had to descend into hell.

And the worst part was, Erin would never know that he loved her.

Chapter Seventeen

Wade ran flat-out toward Mrs. Bester's house, hurdling logs at a dead run, dodging trees and spot fires. The smoke hung low, impeding his visibility, but he didn't dare slow down. The fire could blow up at any time.

His lungs heaving, he gasped in air, then coughed out the hot, choking smoke. He hit a clump of brambles and crashed through, then continued running for his life. The flames roared and snapped behind him, threatening to explode.

Suddenly he broke through the woods to the grassy clearing surrounding the house. Mrs. Bester's car was parked in the driveway, which meant she hadn't left yet. He leaped up the porch steps and pounded the door. "Mrs. Bester!"

He twisted the doorknob and shoved. The unlocked door swung open. "Mrs. Bester!"

He burst into the house and glanced around quickly, then bolted down the hall to the kitchen. Maybe she'd left in another vehicle, but he had to make sure. "Mrs. Bester!"

"Up here."

Adrenaline surged through his nerves and he took the stairs two at a time. Why hadn't she left by now? Didn't the woman have any sense?

"Bitsy," he heard her call. "Come here, Bitsy, come here." He dashed into the bedroom at the top of the stairs. Mrs. Bester lay facedown on the floor beside the bed.

"Come on." He gasped for breath. "The canyon's on fire."

"But Bitsy's under the bed. I can't get her out."

"No time." He reached down and grabbed her arm.

"No!" She pulled back. "I can't leave my cat."

His pulse thundered. "You don't have a choice. The house is about to burn up. Let's go!"

He tugged on her arm again, but she stayed on the floor. "No, not without Bitsy."

Hell. They were going to die because of a cat. He scowled at her in disgust. He wished he could leave her. He'd never liked the woman. She'd made his life miserable growing up and just cost Erin her job.

But like her or not, he had to save her. He strode to the bed and yanked a pillowcase loose. Then he stretched out on the floor and scooted as far under the bed as he could.

A ball of white fur huddled against the wall, its blue eyes slitted in warning. He reached in and the cat hissed. Determined, he caught its leg and tugged. The cat dug its claws in his arm and scratched, burning his skin. "Damn!"

"Be careful," Mrs. Bester cried. "Don't hurt her."

He grunted. He was the one getting injured here. The cat sank its claws in deeper, but he gritted his teeth and pulled it out.

"Bitsy!" Mrs. Bester reached for the cat, but he quickly stuck it into the pillowcase and knotted it shut.

"She'll run off if you try to hold her." He rolled to his feet and shook his hand against the pain, then slung the pillowcase over his shoulder. The cat went wild, thrashing and dancing on his back. He flinched when its claws snagged his shirt. "Come on."

"You can't—"

"The cat's fine. Let's go." Figuring she'd follow the cat, he rushed down the stairs and out the door. Mrs. Bester came up behind him. They both froze.

A wall of red and orange flames headed toward them. The air roared like a rocketing train.

Mrs. Bester turned back to the house. He grabbed her arm and pulled her down the porch steps toward the fire. "This way."

"No." She jerked away and ran for her car.

"Not that way," he yelled. "We've got to get into the black."

The fire made a loud sucking noise. She stumbled and turned, her eyes wild. Huge flames flared up. She screamed and started running again.

He sprinted after her and grabbed her arm. "We can't outrun it. The fire's too fast. We've got to get into the black." And hope to God that the kids burned out that escape route. "This way."

"No!" She pulled against him and fell. Then she scrambled to her feet and lurched forward.

The wind gusted. Sparks blew past and the grass around them ignited. He swung around to look. Damn. If they didn't get into the black, they were going to die right here.

He turned back to Mrs. Bester, but she lay sprawled in the dirt, unconscious. What the hell? A heart attack? His nerves jumping, he dropped to his knee beside her and set down the cat. He lifted her wrist. She had a pulse, so she'd probably just fainted. Did it matter? If he didn't haul her out, she'd die for sure.

His own pulse erratic now, he pulled her to a sitting position, then hefted her over his shoulder in a fireman's carry. He rose to his feet and staggered under her weight, trying to get his balance. The damn woman weighed more than his fire pack and it was killing his knee.

Hurrying now, he scooped up the pillowcase with the cat inside, shifted the weight on his shoulder, then loped toward the path along the canyon wall.

His nerves tightened as the fire whipped toward him, and fear trickled down his spine. He trusted the kids, knew they'd done the best they could. He just hoped it was good enough.

His heart full, he fixed an image of Erin in his mind. The woman he needed. The woman he loved.

And he was going to see her again. He was damn well going to survive now that he finally had someone to live for.

He shifted Mrs. Bester again, gripped the thrashing pillowcase tighter and plunged into the swirling smoke.

* * *

Erin paced the towpath by the river, battling her nerves. Hours had passed since Wade left the house, and there'd been no sign of him or the kids. She'd brought down water and sandwiches, trying to help in some small way, but as the hours passed, her apprehension grew.

She'd had no idea the fire was this big. Smoke drifted across acres of blackened earth. Pumps spewed water through the ashes. She inhaled the stench of charred earth and anxiety clutched at her heart.

People milled around the towpath, but no one had any news. A photographer took shots of the fire. Emergency workers chatted by an ambulance down the path.

She spotted the fireman she'd spoken to earlier and rushed over to stop him. "Have you found them yet?"

He paused, his face grim. "Butch spotted them a while ago near the canyon. He's heading back now to see if he can find out what's going on." He shook his head. "The wind's blowing the fire right toward there."

Suddenly a distant roar filled the air. Black smoke roiled over the tree line.

"Oh, man," he said. "The canyon just went up."

A terrible fear sliced her chest. The canyon was burning. What if they were in there? How could they ever survive?

Oh, God. Her heart shuddered hard with foreboding and she covered her mouth with her hand. She had to find Wade. He might need her. He could be injured! That certainty lodged in her mind.

She turned and started running up the fire line. "Ma'am!" the fireman called. "You can't go up there. It's too dangerous."

She ignored him. When he yelled again, she ran faster, following the trench they had dug. She scrambled through ashes and over tree stumps, past drifting smoke and smoldering logs, her fear building with every second.

The fire roared in the distance and her heart rocketed inside her chest. She prayed that nothing happened to the kids. Or Wade. Oh, God, she couldn't lose Wade.

For an eternity she raced along the jagged trench, fueled by panic and nerves. Stark terror clawed at her heart. Desperation screamed through her mind.

But finally she couldn't run anymore. Her chest heaved and her lungs burned. She braced her hands on her knees and sawed in air.

Just then, Sean came out of the trees toward her, a shovel slung over his shoulder, his face streaked with dirt. The other kids trailed behind him.

A wave of relief swept through her. "Sean!" she cried. Thank goodness they were safe. But they looked so somber. And where was Wade?

A man came out of the woods just then. Her heart leaped, then abruptly plunged. It was Butch Ableson. Her panic mounting, she glanced around. "Where's Wade?"

The kids grouped around her and stopped. "He went after Mrs. Bester," Sean said.

Her heart stalled. Mrs. Bester lived in the canyon. Where the fire had just blown up.

Jay set down the chain saw he carried. Breathing heavily, he wiped the soot from his eyes. "He told us to burn out an escape route for him, then come back down here."

An escape route. She let out a strangled cry.

For several moments no one spoke, not daring to voice the fear. "Wade knows what he's doing," Sean finally said, his voice wavering.

Dread ran through her blood. He knew exactly what he was doing. He was an expert. He knew that fire would explode and that he couldn't survive it.

And he went in anyway. He did the right thing, just as he always had. Even if it cost him his life.

She clutched her mouth. Nausea rose and she trembled violently, wanting to wretch. She thought she'd never survive his rejection.

But nothing compared with the knowledge that he was dead.

Chapter Eighteen

His head down, his eyes burning, Wade jogged through the charred grass with Mrs. Bester slung over his back. His neck and shoulders throbbed, and sweat streamed down his face. He wished to hell she'd come to so they could move faster. He'd had some damned harrowing moments getting through that fire front that he didn't care to relive. Even his eyebrows were singed.

He paused, adjusted his grip on her legs and gritted his teeth. The old battle-ax weighed more than Jake, the smokejumping bro he'd hauled over the mountain after he'd pierced his leg on a stob. And carrying Bitsy didn't help. He grimaced at his shredded forearms.

He choked down another lungful of smoke, coughed, then slugged up the narrow escape route toward the edge of the canyon. Glowing stump holes dotted the charred forest. Embers from the main fire gusted past in the wind. The fire snapped and rushed behind him, urging him on.

At the top of the blackened incline, he paused to catch his breath. His lungs heaved and gritty sweat stung his eyes. Soot covered his clothes and hands, and a dull pain dogged his knee. But he'd made it out of the fire. He was alive and damned grateful for it.

He spared a minute to savor the relief, the exhilaration, then exhaled and started trudging toward the river. Every inch of the jagged fire line testified to the stamina of those kids. They'd never hesitated, never complained, even after digging for hours. His chest swelled with pride and contentment.

And gratitude. He was damned lucky he'd had those kids along. He never would have survived without them.

And he had every reason to live now. *Erin.* His throat squeezed tight and longing seeped through his heart. He ached to see her again. To marry her. To wake up every day for the rest of his life to the sight of those gorgeous green eyes.

But no matter how badly he wanted to blurt out his feelings, he wasn't going to mess this up. She deserved a ring. Romance. A down-on-his-knees proposal.

Oh, yeah. After years of getting it wrong, he was finally going to get this part right.

"Wade!" He looked up, surprised to see that he'd reached the river. Jay waved at him from the crowd and the fist in his chest relaxed. The kids were safe. They'd all made it. He grinned.

Several men ran toward him, snagging his attention. One pushed a camera in his face and he blinked.

"What happened?" They lifted Mrs. Bester from his shoulders and lowered her to the ground.

"I think she just passed out." He rolled his shoulders, then rubbed the knots in his neck. "I got a pulse on her back at the house, but haven't checked since."

"We need a gurney over here!" a man shouted.

"Here." He shoved the bagged cat at the photographer and strode toward the towpath, searching for Erin. The crowd surged around him and blocked his way.

Someone pounded him on the back. "Great job."

"Damned nervy," another man said. "I'm Chief Hancock." He grabbed Wade's hand and pumped it. "I'd like to talk to you when you get a chance."

"Sure." He spared him a quick nod, then continued scanning the crowd. Where was she? His pulse quickened in anticipation.

But then the teens surged around him, whooping and laughing in celebration, and he turned his attention to them. Their eyes were red from the smoke, their teeth flashing white in their grimy faces. He grinned at their exuberance.

His heart light, he gave them all a high-five—Jay and Alex. The new kid, who'd done a hell of a job. But Sean wasn't with the group.

He glanced around, then finally spotted him standing on the fringes, his hands stuffed into his pockets, his eyes huge.

His chest suddenly tight, he strode over and stopped beside him. "Hey." He put his hand on Sean's shoulder. "Thanks for getting me out of there."

"Yeah."

"Thought for a minute I wouldn't make it."

"Me, too," Sean whispered.

"Yeah." He tipped his head back and blinked, then swallowed to ease the ache in his throat. "Damned scary business. Glad I had you hotshots along."

Sean managed a wobbly smile.

"So, you think we're good enough to be hotshots?" Jay asked from behind him.

He turned around and grinned. "Best ones I've ever seen."

The photographer jogged over, minus the cat, and flashed his camera again. "So how does it feel to be a hero?" he asked.

Wade shrugged. "Ask the kids. They did most of the work." The photographer turned to interview Jay and a sense of fulfillment filled him. This felt right. Teaching the kids. Staying in Millstown. Marrying Erin.

Just as Norm would have wanted. Peace settled deep in his gut. Yeah. This was exactly what Norm would have wanted.

His gaze returned to the crowded towpath. He spotted a blaze of red hair and his pulse sped up. Erin turned and their gazes met.

His world narrowed to those dazzling green eyes and a huge surge of warmth filled his heart. How could he have been so blind? How could he have gone all those years and not realized that he loved her? Even Norm had figured it out.

But now he knew. His gaze locked firmly on hers, he strode forward, determined to claim his woman. Erin. The woman he'd always loved.

She sobbed his name and ran toward him, and he

walked straight into her arms. Where he intended to stay forever. Where he belonged.

Erin stood in the sunroom late the next afternoon and gazed out at the solemn sky. Dark clouds hung low over the woods, their steel bottoms blurred against the branches. She pressed her hand against the bubbled glass and sighed at the irony. After all these months, it was finally going to rain.

And Wade was going to leave.

Melancholy settled deep in her stomach, along with a heavy sense of finality. She knew he was going. He hadn't said the words yet, but he'd lain awake all night, preoccupied and restless, hushing her attempts to speak with a kiss.

Her throat thickened. He was right, of course. What was there left to say? Nothing, except goodbye.

He'd left for town early this morning. Taking care of last-minute business, no doubt. Maybe setting up an account for Sean.

She turned her gaze to the newspaper she'd set on the chair and, despite her gloom, a wry smile tugged at her mouth. He'd probably spent the entire time fending off congratulations, now that he'd become a local hero.

The front page of the paper had a large photo of Wade carting Mrs. Bester to safety, with that heart-stopping grin on his face. The entire first section contained articles about the fire, the drought, Wade and smokejumping, plus photos of him with the teens.

She wondered how he was handling the change—going from pariah to hero overnight. Knowing Wade, he probably didn't much care.

The Harley's low pulse reached her ears just then, and her heart jerked to a halt. He was back. Oh, God. Now she had to say goodbye.

Barely breathing, she waited. Seconds later he limped into view outside the sunroom and a huge lump formed in her throat. She knew she'd remember this moment forever, of Wade in his faded jeans, his chestnut hair gleaming in the dusty light. Those wide shoulders that rescued the world encased in his soft leather jacket.

He opened the door and his somber brown eyes met hers. For a moment he didn't move, didn't speak. Her pulse throbbed loud in her ears.

"Want to go for a walk?" he finally asked.

His deep voice rumbled through her nerves and her heart lurched with sudden panic. She wanted to run and hide. To delay what she knew had to happen. Oh, Lord, she couldn't face this.

But that wasn't fair to Wade. With cold dread gripping her heart, she nodded, grabbed her sweater and pulled it over her head, then followed him out the door.

"Let's go down by the river."

"All right." They walked in silence. Their shoes crunched over the gravel. Dry leaves scattered in front of them in the breeze. Moisture hung strong in the air, indicating that rain was near.

And so was the end of their relationship. Feeling as if she were heading to the gallows instead of the river, she walked beside him to the ruined mill, then onto a grassy clearing. He stopped beside a large rock.

"You remember this place?"

"Of course." How could she forget it? They'd first made love here in the grass, all those years ago.

And it was the perfect place to say farewell. He walked over and perched on the boulder, then held out his hand for her to join him. Her heart raw, she grasped his hand and sat.

Unable to meet his gaze, she stared at his worn boots. She listened to the wind sigh overhead. The river swirl against the rocks. Felt the rough strength of his hand. And a sickening rush of despair.

"I've always wondered about that night," he continued. "Why you came to me, I mean."

She thought back to that hot, wild evening. "I knew you were leaving," she confessed. "And I wanted to make love to you before you left."

"But why me?" he asked again.

She raised her gaze to his. And saw the boy who'd always understood her. The wounded, vulnerable child who'd protected her from his fate, not asking anything in return. The man who even now would give her everything he owned, or do anything she asked. The generous, sexy man she'd loved forever.

She swallowed hard. "I just... I wanted you to be the one. Because I loved you."

He didn't answer. But she saw that look in his eyes again and her heart climbed high in her chest. She hardly breathed when he reached out and tucked a strand of hair behind her ear.

"I was so scared that you'd turn me down," she whispered.

A crooked grin slashed his face. "Not a chance. I'd been fantasizing about you for years."

"Really?"

"Oh, yeah. I staggered around with chronic sleep deprivation, thanks to you."

She squeezed his hand gratefully, knowing he was trying to lighten the mood. To save her from the embarrassment of not being loved back. Dear Wade. Still protecting her. A fierce warmth surged through her heart.

"I didn't sleep much last night, either," he said suddenly.

Her heart abruptly plummeted. "I know."

"I thought about a lot of things," he continued. "My job, the future. What matters to me, and what I need to do."

"I understand," she whispered.

"Yeah. You always did." He cradled her hand between his. "You were the only one."

"That's not true. Norm understood you, too."

"Yeah, you're right. He did." To her surprise, he chuckled. "Maybe too well."

He let go of her hand and pulled a flat, square box from his jacket pocket. "I got you something."

A farewell gift. Oh, God. A horrible ache gripped her heart. "Wade, I…"

"It's not much, I know, but I still want you to have it." His voice lowered. "Please?"

Her vision blurring, she nodded. He needed to give her something for closure, to reconcile the past. To ease his conscience.

Her hands trembling, she opened the box. And her breath lodged in her throat. A glittering diamond and emerald necklace nestled against the satin lining, alongside matching earrings. "Oh, Wade, you shouldn't have…"

"The green matches your eyes," he explained. "At least, that's the color they turn when you're mad." His voice got husky. "Or in bed."

Her throat clammed shut. Tears welled in her eyes. She struggled not to sob her despair.

He lifted the necklace out of the box. "Move your hair so I can put it on."

She pulled her hair to the side and he draped it around her throat. His big fingers felt warm against her neck as he fumbled with the tiny clasp.

Then his fingers slid along the necklace to the lowest stone and he settled it between her breasts. "I pictured you in this," he said, his voice gruff. "But without the sweater."

Despite her efforts, tears traced a path down her cheeks and her desperation surged. She didn't care about her pride. She wanted to flat-out beg him to stay.

"Wade, I—" She stopped. She couldn't do that to him. Not Wade. No matter how badly she wanted to keep him, she had to let him move on. Just as she had once before.

But this time would destroy her.

She swallowed hard, feeling completely shredded inside. "Thank you."

His whiskey-brown gaze held hers. He looked serious, almost vulnerable, and he sat perfectly still. "There's something else that goes with it."

A bracelet, no doubt. She sniffed and wiped her cheeks with the heel of her hands. Lord, she didn't know how she'd survive this. Why was he dragging it out?

He fumbled in his pocket, then pulled out a small, velvet box. *Too small to hold a bracelet.*

Their gazes latched and suddenly she couldn't breathe. He set the box in her palm. Her heart slammed against her chest as she clutched it. Blood rushed hard in her ears.

"Open it," he whispered.

Trembling, she tore her gaze from his. She flipped open the box and gasped. Inside was a huge diamond ring.

Her world tilted.

"Marry me, Erin. I need you."

Her eyes brimmed and he grasped her arms. "I love you," he whispered. "Good God, I love you."

Her vision blurred. A sob escaped her. She threw her arms around his strong neck.

"Don't make me suffer," he said, his voice rough in her ear. "Tell me if that's a yes."

She struggled to choke out the sound. "Yes!"

In one fluid motion he rose, still holding her in his arms. He twirled her slowly around, then captured her lips with his. He moved his mouth hard over hers, blazing, searing and possessing. With a kiss of affirmation and promise. Of love. From her best friend, her soul mate. Her lover. He loved her! Her heart threatened to burst.

She clung to him, kissing him fervently, while hot tears leaked from her eyes. She wanted him closer, harder. As if she could absorb him into her skin. And never let him go.

After an eternity he broke away. He eased back slightly, his expression serious, and took the small box from her hand. Then, his gaze locked on hers, he lifted her shaking hand and inched the ring over her finger. His Adam's apple dipped.

"I love you," he said, his voice gruff. "I always have. I don't know how I never saw that.

"Or maybe I did. I think I knew it that night, and it scared me to death. I told myself I was doing you a favor by leaving, but I was really a coward." His dark gaze pleaded with hers. "Can you forgive me?"

Her heart swelled. Her wonderful, stubborn hero. Tears streaked from her eyes and she sniffed. "Only if I can pay off Norm's loan."

The edges of his mouth kicked up. "Not a chance."

He pulled her close again, and for an eternity, held her tight. She closed her eyes and rested against him, a profound peace filling her heart. Feeling his strength, his solid warmth. Feeling exactly right.

But they still had unfinished business. She reluctantly lifted her head. "About your job..."

His big hand stroked her back. "I've already got that covered. Chief Hancock offered me a job. The pay's not great to start, but the hours sound right, and I can take his job when he retires."

"No." Married or not, she wouldn't trap him. "I want you to keep on smokejumping. Really. I don't mind if you do it. It suits you, Wade. You were wonderful on that fire.

"Besides," she said. "I don't teach in the summer, so I can always fly out and see you."

He reached up and smoothed a strand of hair from her face. "I thought about that. And maybe I could do it for a year or two, but eventually, my knee's going to go.

"And I'll be busy here. Working, fixing up the house with Sean. In fact, I thought maybe we could take in foster kids, since we've got that whole third floor. If you wouldn't mind."

Her heart softened and swelled. What a perfect thing to do. "I'd like that. But are you sure?"

"Yeah, I'm sure. I spent the whole night planning it out." His voice dropped to a husky whisper. "And I'm hoping we can make some kids of our own. In fact, I'd like to spend a lot of time doing that."

Her breath caught. "You want kids?"

"Oh, yeah." Heat flashed in his eyes. "As many as we can have. I figure a half-dozen Winslows should terrorize the town pretty good."

A family. Hot need slinked through her veins. "Exactly when do you want to get started?"

"How about now?"

"Here?"

"We did it here once before."

The memory made her face heat. "If I remember correctly, it was more than once."

He gave her a wicked grin. "I think I can still match that. Trust me?"

Her heart swelled. "I always have."

Epilogue

"**Y**ou ready?" Wade's best man, Cade McKenzie, asked as they waited in the room behind the altar.

"Hell, I've been ready for weeks." He'd wanted to marry Erin the same day he proposed, but she'd insisted on a formal wedding.

And God knew, he'd do anything that woman asked.

"Thanks again for standing up for me," he added. He knew this was tough for McKenzie. Unable to live with a smokejumper, his wife had left him years back, making him deeply cynical about marriage. Yet, like a true bro, he'd put aside his bitterness to support Wade now.

"I wouldn't have missed this for anything." McKenzie grinned. "I had to see what miracle got you to quit jumping."

A deep warmth spread through his heart at the

thought of Erin. "She's a miracle, all right." And he still couldn't believe that she loved him.

Just then the door swung open and Jay stepped in. "The minister says it's time."

"Finally." Now he could get this ceremony over with and claim his bride. His patience thinning, he followed Jay out the door.

He strode to his designated place across from Grandma, who sat in a wheelchair clutching a huge bouquet of roses. Flickering candles and flame-red poinsettias framed the marble altar behind them. The stained-glass windows along the old stone walls were dark, while outside, the first winter snow muffled Millstown, turning the packed church into a refuge for the community.

And making it a place of magic, of miracles. He inhaled the scent of pine boughs and warm wax, and his anticipation grew. The real miracle was that Erin would soon be his wife.

If only Norm could see it. Sorrow slunk through his heart, along with a surge of assurance. He didn't know much about Heaven, but he knew Norm was definitely in it, looking down on the church and feeling pleased.

Life was good, all right. He scanned the front pew, where the other smokejumpers slumped, hung over, and his mouth curved into a grin. Millstown might never recover from their wild antics, but he'd never known better men.

His throat tightened. He'd been as impressed as hell that they'd come to his wedding, though he would have done the same for them. They shared a bond, these smokejumping bros. They were men like himself, loners banding together to battle fire and fight their private demons.

Except that he got lucky and conquered his.

Or maybe Erin had slain his for him.

His gaze shifted to Jay, who now sat with the smokejumpers on the hard pew. He'd be one of them soon. McKenzie had already phoned a friend and secured a place for him on a hotshot crew.

A commotion at the back of the church caught his attention. His heart jerked, but it was only Mrs. Bester charging up the aisle, her stiff beehive hairdo stacked high. Sean trailed her, trying to offer his arm. Ignoring him, she slid into a pew behind the smokejumpers on the groom's side of the church.

A grin pulled at his mouth. He couldn't believe how much she'd changed since the fire. She'd become his staunchest defender, bragging about him to the town. She'd even convinced the school board to create a new position for Erin at the public high school.

Sean caught his eye and shrugged, then slid into the pew next to Jay. Even Sean had changed, he mused. For once his pants didn't drag on the floor.

Suddenly the music paused and he saw a movement at the vestibule door. A hush fell over the crowd and everyone turned to look.

Erin emerged and his heart stalled. Her gown shimmered in the soft light, all pearls and cream-colored satin. Her red hair blazed beneath her lace veil.

He struggled to breathe. God, she was beautiful, like a vision, the most gorgeous woman he'd ever seen. And she was perfect, inside and out. She was generous, kind, loving. And her passion incinerated his soul.

Their gazes latched and his throat blocked up. His world receded to this one woman as she glided toward him up the aisle.

Erin, the woman he'd always loved. He didn't know how he'd ever deserved her.

His heart full, he stepped down to the aisle to meet her. She stopped beside him and placed her trembling hand on his arm. He clasped his hand firmly over hers and held it next to his heart, right where it belonged. And vowed to never let her go.

* * * * *

Look for Gail Barrett's exciting new novel,
FACING THE FIRE,
available in April 2006
from Silhouette Intimate Moments.

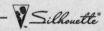

A bear ate my ex, and that's okay.

Stacy Kavanaugh is convinced
that her ex's recent disappearance
in the mountains is the worst
thing that can happen to her.
In the next two weeks, she'll
discover how wrong she really is!

Grin and Bear It
Leslie LaFoy

Home For The Holidays!

Receive a FREE Christmas Collection
containing 4 books by bestselling authors

Harlequin American Romance and Silhouette Special Edition invite you to celebrate Home For The Holidays by offering you this exclusive offer valid only in Harlequin American Romance and Silhouette Special Edition books this November.

To receive your FREE Christmas Collection, send us 3 (three) proofs of purchase of Harlequin American Romance or Silhouette Special Edition books to the addresses below.

In the U.S.:	In Canada:
Home For The Holidays	Home For The Holidays
P.O. Box 9057	P.O. Box 622
Buffalo, NY	Fort Erie, ON
14269-9057	L2A 5X3

- ✂

098 KKI DXJM

_____

Name (PLEASE PRINT)

_____

Address   Apt. #

_____

City   State/Prov.   Zip/Postal Code

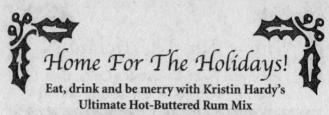

Home For The Holidays!

Eat, drink and be merry with Kristin Hardy's Ultimate Hot-Buttered Rum Mix

Treats make the holiday bright

One of my favorite holiday treats is hot-buttered rum.
Not just any old hot-buttered rum, though. This is the
ultimate, as revered by J. J. Cooper in *Under the Mistletoe*
(Special Edition, December 2005). You'll be seeing
J.J. again, so keep an eye out for him.

Hot Buttered Rum Mix

1 lb butter	*dash salt*
1 lb white sugar	*1 qt light cream*
1 lb brown sugar	*1 tsp vanilla*

add:

Hot Buttered Rum

1 tbsp Hot-Buttered Rum Mix
1 shot dark rum (Myers is good)
Hot water

Cream butter, sugar and salt until emulsified. You want
it light and fluffy, as if making a cake, so don't rush.
Combine cream and vanilla. Add about a half cup at a
time and let blend in thoroughly before adding more. It
should have the consistency of buttercream at the end.
Makes about four cups.

To make hot-buttered rum, add the hot-buttered rum
mix and a shot of dark rum (I like Myers) to a mug. Fill
the rest of the way with hot water. Delicious.

Note:

This recipe makes enough to share. I put it in glass jars with a
pretty label on the front with directions and a ribbon around
the lid. It's an instant holiday gift, and one that almost everyone
will love. For more recipes, go to www.kristinhardy.com.

Home For The Holidays!

While there are many variations of this recipe, here is Tina Leonard's favorite!

GOURMET REINDEER POOP

Mix 1/2 cup butter, 2 cups granulated sugar, 1/2 cup milk and 2 tsp cocoa together in a large saucepan.

Bring to a boil, stirring constantly; boil for 1 minute.

Remove from heat and stir in 1/2 cup peanut butter, 3 cups oatmeal (not instant) and 1/2 cup chopped nuts (optional).

Drop by teaspoon full (larger or smaller as desired) onto wax paper and let harden.

They will set in about 30-60 minutes.

These will keep for several days without refrigerating, up to 2 weeks refrigerated and 2-3 months frozen.

Pack into resealable sandwich bags and attach the following note to each bag.

I woke up with such a scare when I heard Santa call…
"Now dash away, dash away, dash away all!"
I ran to the lawn and in the snowy white drifts,
those nasty reindeer had left "little gifts."
I got an old shovel and started to scoop,
neat little piles of "Reindeer Poop!"
But to throw them away seemed such a waste,
so I saved them, thinking you might like a taste!
As I finished my task, which took quite a while,
Old Santa passed by and he sheepishly smiled.
And I heard him exclaim as he was in the sky…
"Well, they're not potty trained, but at least they can fly!"

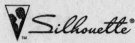

COMING NEXT MONTH